'Ruth Rendell has quite simply transformed the genre of crime writing. She displays her peerless skill in blending the mundane, commonplace aspects of life with the potent murky impulses of desire and greed, obsession and fear' *Sunday Times*

'A brilliant piece of exhumation' *Observer*

'Cleverly plotted and conspicuously well written' *Daily Telegraph*

'Wonderful at exploring the dark corners of the human mind, and the way private fantasies can clash and explode into terrifying violence' *Daily Mail*

'Superb plotting and psychological insight make this another Rendell gripper' *Woman & Home*

'An unusual detective story ... intelligent, well written, with a surprising twist at the end' *Times Literary Supplement*

'England's premier detective-thriller writer' *Spectator*

'Intricate and ingenious' *Yorkshire Post*

'Unguessable and brilliant' *Listener*

'The best mystery writer anywhere in the English-speaking world' *Boston Globe*

OMNIBUSES: COLLECTED SHORT STORIES | COLLECTED STORIES 2 | WEXFORD: AN OMNIBUS | THE SECOND WEXFORD OMNIBUS | THE THIRD WEXFORD OMNIBUS | THE FOURTH WEXFORD OMNIBUS | THE FIFTH WEXFORD OMNIBUS | THREE CASES FOR CHIEF INSPECTOR WEXFORD | THE RUTH RENDELL OMNIBUS | THE SECOND RUTH RENDELL OMNIBUS | THE THIRD RUTH RENDELL OMNIBUS | **CHIEF INSPECTOR WEXFORD NOVELS:** FROM DOON WITH DEATH | A NEW LEASE OF DEATH | WOLF TO THE SLAUGHTER | THE BEST MAN TO DIE | A GUILTY THING SURPRISED | NO MORE DYING THEN | MURDER BEING ONCE DONE

ALSO BY RUTH RENDELL

| SOME LIE AND SOME DIE | SHAKE HANDS FOR EVER | A SLEEPING LIFE | PUT ON BY CUNNING | THE SPEAKER OF MANDARIN | AN UNKINDNESS OF RAVENS | THE VEILED ONE | KISSING THE GUNNER'S DAUGHTER | SIMISOLA | ROAD RAGE | HARM DONE | THE BABES IN THE WOOD | END IN TEARS | NOT IN THE FLESH | THE MONSTER IN THE BOX | **SHORT STORIES:** THE FALLEN CURTAIN | MEANS OF EVIL | THE FEVER TREE | THE NEW GIRLFRIEND | THE COPPER PEACOCK | BLOOD LINES | PIRANHA TO SCURFY | **NOVELLAS:** HEARTSTONES | THE THIEF | **NON-FICTION:** RUTH RENDELL'S SUFFOLK | RUTH RENDELL'S ANTHOLOGY OF THE MURDEROUS MIND | **NOVELS:** TO FEAR A PAINTED DEVIL | VANITY DIES HARD | THE SECRET HOUSE OF DEATH | ONE ACROSS, TWO DOWN | THE FACE OF TRESPASS | A DEMON IN MY VIEW | A JUDGEMENT IN STONE | MAKE DEATH LOVE ME | THE LAKE OF DARKNESS | MASTER OF THE MOOR | THE KILLING DOLL | THE TREE OF HANDS | LIVE FLESH | TALKING TO STRANGE MEN | THE BRIDESMAID | GOING WRONG | THE CROCODILE BIRD | THE KEYS TO THE STREET | A SIGHT FOR SORE EYES | ADAM AND EVE AND PINCH ME | THE ROTTWEILER | THIRTEEN STEPS DOWN | THE WATER'S LOVELY | PORTOBELLO

ruth
rendell

SHAKE HANDS
FOR EVER

arrow books

Reissued by Arrow Books 2010

8 10 9 7

First published in Great Britain in 1975 by
Hutchinson

This edition was first published in paperback in 1976 by Arrow Books
Random House, 20 Vauxhall Bridge Road,
London SW1V 2SA

www.randomhouse.co.uk

Addresses for companies within The Random House Group Limited can be
found at: www.randomhouse.co.uk/offices.htm

The Random House Group Limited Reg. No. 954009

A CIP catalogue record for this book
is available from the British Library

ISBN 9780099534884

Typeset by Replika Press Pvt Ltd, India

Penguin Random House is committed to a sustainable future for
our business, our readers and our planet. This book is made from
Forest Stewardship Council® certified paper.

Printed and bound in Great Britain by Clays Ltd, St Ives plc

*For my aunts, Jenny Waldorff, Laura Winfield,
Margot Richards and Phyllis Ridgway,
with my love.*

1

The woman standing under the departures board at Victoria station had a flat rectangular body and an iron-hard rectangular face. A hat of fawn-coloured corrugated felt rather like a walnut shell encased her head, her hands were gloved in fawn-coloured cotton, and at her feet was the durable but scarcely used brown leather suitcase she had taken on her honeymoon forty-five years before. Her eyes scanned the scurrying commuters while her mouth grew more and more set, the lips thinning to a hairline crack.

She was waiting for her son. He was one minute late and his unpunctuality had begun to afford her a glowing satisfaction. She was hardly aware of this pleasure and, had she been accused of it, would have denied it, just as she would have denied the delight all failure and backsliding in other people brought her. But it was present as an undefined sense of well-being that was to vanish almost as soon as it had been born and be succeeded on Robert's sudden hasty arrival by her usual ill-temper. He was so nearly on time as to make any remarks about his lateness absurd, so she contented herself with offering her leathery cheek to his lips and saying:

'There you are then.'

'Have you got your ticket?' said Robert Hathall.

She hadn't. She knew that money had been tight with him for the three years of his second marriage, but that was his fault. Paying her share would only encourage him.

'You'd better go and get them,' she said, 'unless you want us to miss the train,' and she held even more tightly to her zipped-up handbag.

He was a long time about it. She noted that the Eastbourne train, stopping at Toxborough, Myringham and Kingsmarkham, was due to depart at six-twelve, and it was five past now. No fully formed uncompromising thought that it would be nice to miss the train entered her mind, any more than she had consciously told herself it would be nice to find her daughter-in-law in tears, the house filthy and no meal cooked, but once more the seeds of pleasurable resentment began germinating. She had looked forward to this weekend with a deep contentment, certain it would go wrong. Nothing would suit her better than that it should begin to go wrong by their arriving late through no fault of hers, and that their lateness should result in a quarrel between Robert and Angela. But all this smouldered silent and unanalysed under her immediate awareness that Robert was making a mess of things again.

Nevertheless, they caught the train. It was crowded and they both had to stand. Mrs Hathall never complained. She would have fainted before citing her age and her varicose veins as reasons why this or that man should give up his seat to her. Stoicism governed her. Instead, she planted her thick body which, buttoned up in a stiff fawn coat, had the appearance of a wardrobe, in such a way as to prevent the passenger in the window seat from moving his legs or reading his newspaper. She had only one thing to say to Robert and that could keep till there were fewer listeners, and she found it hard to suppose he could have anything to say to her. Hadn't they, after all, spent every weekday evening together for the past two months? But people, she had noticed with some puzzlement, were prone to chatter when they had nothing to say. Even her own son was guilty of this. She listened grimly while he went on about the beautiful scenery through which they would soon pass, the amenities of Bury Cottage, and how much Angela was looking forward to seeing her. Mrs Hathall permitted herself a kind of snort at this last, a two-syllabled grunt made somewhere in her glottis that could be roughly interpreted as a laugh. Her lips didn't move. She was reflecting on the one and only time she had met her daughter-in-law, in that room in Earls Court, when Angela had committed the outrage of referring to Eileen as a greedy bitch. Much would have to be done, many amends be made, before that indiscretion could be forgotten. Mrs Hathall remembered how she had marched straight out of that room and down the stairs, resolving never – never under any circumstances – to see Angela again. It only proved how forbearing she was that she was going to Kingsmarkham now.

At Myringham the passenger by the window, his legs numb, staggered out of the train and Mrs Hathall got his seat. Robert, she could tell, was getting nervous. There was nothing surprising in that. He knew very well this Angela couldn't compete with Eileen as cook and housekeeper and he was wondering just how far below his first wife's standards his second would fall. His next words confirmed her conviction that this was troubling his mind.

'Angela's spent the week spring-cleaning the place to make it nice for you.'

Mrs Hathall was shocked that anyone could make such a statement aloud and in front of a carriage full of people. What she would have liked to say was, firstly, that he should keep his voice down and, secondly, that any decent woman kept her house clean at all times. But she contented herself with a 'I'm sure she needn't put herself out for me' and added repressively that it was time he got her suitcase down.

'It's five minutes yet,' said Robert.

She replied by getting heavily to her feet and struggling with the case herself. Robert and another man intervened to help her, the case nearly fell on to the head of a girl with a baby in her arms, and by the time the train drew to a halt at Kingsmarkham, sending them all staggering and clutching each other, the carriage was in a small uproar.

Out on the platform, Mrs Hathall said, 'That could have been avoided if you'd done as you were asked. You always were obstinate.'

She couldn't understand why he didn't retaliate and fight back. He must be more strung-up than she had thought. To goad him further, she said, 'I suppose we're going to have a taxi?'

'Angela's meeting us in the car.'

Then there wasn't much time for her to say what she had to. She pushed her suitcase at him and took hold of his arm in a proprietary manner. It wasn't that she needed his support or his reassurance, but she felt it essential that this daughter-in-law – how galling and disreputable to have two daughters-in-law! – should, in her first glimpse of them, see them consolidated and arm-in-arm.

'Eileen came in this morning,' she said as they gave up their tickets.

He shrugged absently. 'I wonder you two don't live together.'

'That'd make things easy for you. You wouldn't have to keep a roof over her head.' Mrs Hathall tightened her grip on the arm which he had attempted to jerk away. 'She said to give you her love and say why don't you go round one evening while you're in London.'

'You must be joking,' said Robert Hathall, but he

said it vaguely and without much rancour. He was scanning the car park.

Pursuing her theme, Mrs Hathall began, 'It's a wicked shame ...' and then stopped in mid-sentence. A marvellous realization was dawning on her. She knew that car of Robert's, would know it anywhere, he'd had it long enough thanks to the straits that women had brought him to. She too let her sharp eyes rove round the tarmac square, and then she said in a satisfied tone, 'Doesn't look as if she'd put herself out to meet us.'

Robert seemed discomfited. 'The train was a couple of minutes early.'

'It was three minutes late,' said his mother. She sighed happily. Eileen would have been there to meet them all right. Eileen would have been on the platform with a kiss for her mother-in-law and a cheerful promise of the nice tea that awaited them. And her grand-daughter too ... Mrs Hathall remarked as if to herself but loud enough to be heard, 'Poor little Rosemary.'

It was very unlike Robert, who was his mother's son, to take this sort of aggravation without comment, but again he made none. 'It doesn't matter,' he said. 'It's not all that far.'

'I can walk,' said Mrs Hathall in the stoical tone of one who realizes that there will be worse trials to come and that the first and lightest must be bravely borne. 'I'm quite used to walking.'

Their journey took them up the station approach and Station Road, across Kingsmarkham High Street and along the Stowerton Road. It was a fine

September evening, the air aglow with sunset light, the trees heavily foliaged, the gardens bright with the last and finest flowers of summer. But Mrs Hathall, who might have said like the lover in the ballad, 'What are the beauties of nature to me?', disregarded it all. Her wistfulness had given way to certainty. Robert's depression could mean only one thing. This wife of his, this thief, this breaker of a happy marriage, was going to let him down and he knew it.

They turned into Wool Lane, a narrow tree-shaded byway without a pavement. 'That's what I call a nice house,' said Mrs Hathall.

Robert glanced at the detached, between-the-wars villa. 'It's the only one down here apart from ours. A woman called Lake lives there. She's a widow.'

'Pity it's not yours,' said his mother with a wealth of implication. 'Is it much further?'

'Round the next bend. I can't think what's happened to Angela.' He looked at her uneasily. 'I'm sorry about this, Mother. I really am sorry.'

She was so amazed that he should depart from family tradition as actually to apologize for anything, that she could make no answer to this and remained silent until the cottage came into view. A slight disappointment marred her satisfaction, for this was a house, a decent though old house of brown brick with a neat slate roof. 'Is this it?'

He nodded and opened the gate for her. Mrs Hathall observed that the garden was untended, the flower-beds full of weeds and the grass inches high. Under a neglected-looking tree lay a scattering of rotten plums. She said, 'Hmm,' a non-committal noise characteristic of her and signifying that things were turning out the way she expected. He put the key in the front-door lock and the door swung open. 'Come along in, Mother.'

He was certainly upset now. There was no mistaking it. She knew that way he had of compressing his lips while a little muscle worked in his left cheek. And there was a harsh nervous note in his voice as he called out, 'Angela, we're here!'

Mrs Hathall followed him into the living room. She could hardly believe her eyes. Where were the dirty teacups, finger-marked gin glasses, scattered clothes, crumbs and dust? She planted herself rectangularly on the spotless carpet and turned slowly round, scrutinizing the ceiling for cobwebs, the windows for smears, the ashtrays for that forgotten cigarette end. A strange uncomfortable chill took hold of her. She felt like a champion who, confident of victory, certain of her own superiority, loses the first set to a tyro.

Robert came back and said, 'I can't think where Angela's got to. She's not in the garden. I'll just go into the garage and see if the car's there. Would you like to go on upstairs, Mother? Your bedroom's the big one at the back.'

Having ascertained that the dining-room table wasn't laid and that there was no sign of preparations for a meal in the immaculate kitchen where the rubber gloves and dusting gloves of household labour lay beside the sink, Mrs Hathall mounted the stairs. She ran one finger along the picture rail on the landing. Not a mark, the woodwork might have been newly painted. The bedroom which was to be hers was as exquisitely clean as the rest of the house, the bed turned down to show candy-striped sheets, one dressing-table drawer open and lined with tissue paper. She noted it all but never once, as one revelation followed another, did she allow this evidence of Angela's excellence to mitigate her hatred. It was a pity that her daughter-in-law should have armed herself with this weapon, a pity and that was all. No doubt her other faults, such as this one of not being here to greet her, would more than compensate for this small virtue.

Mrs Hathall went into the bathroom. Polished enamel, clean fluffy towels, guest soap ... She set her mouth grimly. Money couldn't have been as tight as Robert made out. She told herself only that she resented his deception, not putting even into thought-words that she was confronting a second deprivation, that of not being able to throw their poverty and the reason for it in their faces. She washed her hands and came out on to the landing. The door to the main bedroom was slightly ajar. Mrs Hathall hesitated. But the temptation to take a look inside and perhaps find a tumbled bed, a mess of squalid cosmetics, was too great to resist. She entered the room carefully.

The bed wasn't tumbled but neatly made. On top of the covers lay a girl face-downwards, apparently deeply asleep. Her dark, rather shaggy, hair lay spread over her shoulders and her left arm was flung out. Mrs Hathall said, 'Hmm,' all her warm pleasure welling back unalloyed. Robert's wife was lying asleep, perhaps even drunk. She hadn't bothered to take off her canvas shoes before collapsing there and she was dressed exactly as she had been that day in Earls Court, probably as she always dressed, in shabby faded blue jeans and a red check shirt. Mrs Hathall thought of Eileen's pretty afternoon dresses and short permed hair, of Eileen who would only have slept in the daytime if she had been at death's door, and then she went over to the bed and stared down, frowning. 'Hmm,' she said again, but this time it was a 'Hmm' of admonition, designed to announce her presence and get an immediate shamed response.

There was none. The genuine anger of the person who feels herself unbearably slighted seized Mrs Hathall. She put her hand on her daughter-in-law's shoulder to shake it. But she didn't shake it. The flesh of that neck was icy cold, and as she lifted the veil of hair, she saw a pallid cheek, swollen and bluish.

Most women would have screamed. Mrs Hathall made no sound. Her body became a little more set and cupboard-like as she drew herself upright and placed her thick large hand to her palpitating heart. Many times in her long life she had seen death, her parents', her husband's, uncles', aunts', but she had never before seen what the purplish mark on that neck showed – death by violence. No thought of triumph came to her and no fear. She felt nothing but shock. Heavily, she plodded across the room and began to descend the stairs.

Robert was waiting at the foot of them. In so far as she was capable of love, she loved him, and in going up to him and placing her hand on his arm, she addressed him in a muted reluctant voice, the nearest she could get to tenderness. And she used the only words she knew for breaking this kind of bad news.

'There's been an accident. You'd best go up and see for yourself. It's – it's too late to do anything. Try and take it like a man.'

He stood quite still. He didn't speak.

'She's gone, Robert, your wife's dead.' She repeated the words because he didn't seem to take them in. 'Angela's dead, son.'

A vague uncomfortable feeling came over her that she ought to embrace him, speak some tender word, but she had long ago forgotten how. Besides, she was shaking now and her heart was pumping irregularly. He had neither paled nor flushed. Steadily he walked past her and mounted the stairs. She waited there, impotent, awe-stricken, rubbing her hands together and hunching her shoulders. Then he called out from above in a harsh but calm voice:

'Phone the police, Mother, and tell them what's happened.'

She was glad of something to do, and finding the phone on a low table under a bookshelf, she set her finger to the nine slot in the dial.

2

He was a tall man, carrying insufficient weight for
his wide frame. And he had an unhealthy look,
his belly sagging a little, his skin a mottled red.
Though still black, his hair was thinning and dry,
and his features were bold and harsh. He sat in an
armchair, slumped as if he had been injured and then
flung there. By contrast, his mother sat upright, her
solid legs pressed close together, her hands palm-
downwards on her lap, her hard eyes fixed on her
son with more of sternness than sympathy.

Chief Inspector Wexford thought of those Spartan
mothers who preferred seeing their sons brought
home on their shields to knowing they were taken
captive. He wouldn't have been surprised if she had
told this man to pull himself together, but she hadn't

yet uttered a word or made any sign to himself and Inspector Burden beyond giving them a curt nod when admitting them to the house. She looked, he thought, like an old-style prison wardress or mistress of a workhouse.

From upstairs the footfalls of other policemen could be heard, passing to and fro. The woman's body had been photographed where it lay, had been identified by the widower and removed to the mortuary. But the men still had much to do. The house was being examined for fingerprints, for the weapon, for some clue as to how this girl had met her death. And it was a big house for a cottage, with five good-sized rooms apart from the kitchen and the bathroom. They had been there since eight and now it was nearly midnight.

Wexford, who stood by a table on which lay the dead woman's driving licence, purse and the other contents of her handbag, was examining her passport. It identified her as a British subject, born in Melbourne, Australia, thirty-two years old, occupation housewife, hair dark brown, eyes grey, height five feet five inches, no distinguishing marks. Angela Margaret Hathall. The passport was three years old and had never been used to pass any port. The photograph in it bore about as much resemblance to the dead woman as such photographs usually bear to their subjects.

'Your wife lived alone here during the week, Mr Hathall?' he said, moving away from the table and sitting down.

Hathall nodded. He answered in a low voice

not much above a whisper. 'I used to work in Toxborough. When I got a new job in London I couldn't travel up and down. That was in July. I've been living with my mother during the week, coming home for weekends.'

'You and your mother arrived here at seven-thirty, I think?'

'Twenty past,' said Mrs Hathall, speaking for the first time. She had a harsh metallic voice. Under the South London accent lay a hint of North Country origins.

'So you hadn't seen your wife since – when? Last Sunday? Monday?'

'Sunday night,' said Hathall. 'I went to my mother's by train on Sunday night. My – Angela drove me to the station. I – I phoned her every day. I phoned her today. At lunchtime. She was all right.' He made a breath-catching sound like a sob, and his body swayed forward. 'Who – who would have done this? Who would have wanted to kill – *Angela*?'

The words had a stagey ring, a false sound, as if they had been learned from some television play or cliché-ridden thriller. But Wexford knew that grief can sometimes only be expressed in platitudes. We are original in our happy moments. Sorrow has only one voice, one cry.

He answered the question in similarly hackneyed words. 'That's what we have to find out, Mr Hathall. You were at work all day?'

'Marcus Flower, Public Relations Consultants. Half Moon Street. I'm an accountant.' Hathall cleared his throat. 'You can check with them that I was there all day.'

Wexford didn't quite raise his eyebrows. He stroked his chin and looked at the man in silence. Burden's face gave nothing away, but he could tell the inspector was thinking the same thought as his own. And during this silence Hathall, who had uttered this last sentence almost with eagerness, gave a louder sob and buried his face in his hands.

Rigid as stone, Mrs Hathall said, 'Don't give way, son. Bear it like a man.'

But I must feel it like a man … As the bit from *Macbeth* came into Wexford's mind, he wondered fleetingly why he felt so little sympathy for Hathall, why he wasn't moved. Was he getting the way he'd always sworn he wouldn't get? Was he getting hard and indifferent at last? Or was there really something false in the man's behaviour that gave the lie to these sobs and this abandonment to grief? Probably he was just tired, reading meanings where there was none; probably the woman had picked up a stranger and that stranger had killed her. He waited till Hathall had taken his hands away and raised his face.

'Your car is missing?'

'It was gone from the garage when I got home.' There were no tears on the hard thin cheeks. Would a son of that flint-faced woman be capable of squeezing out tears?

'I'll want a description of your car and its number. Sergeant Martin will get the details from you in a minute.' Wexford got up. 'The doctor has given you a sedative, I believe. I suggest you take it and try and get some sleep. In the morning I should like to talk to you again, but there's very little more we can do tonight.'

Mrs Hathall shut the door on them in the manner of one snapping 'Not today, thanks' at a couple of hawkers. For a moment or two Wexford stood on the path, surveying the place. Light from the bedroom windows showed him a couple of lawns that hadn't been mown for months and a bare plum tree. The path was paved but the drive which ran between the house wall and the right-hand fence was a strip of concrete.

'Where's this garage he was talking about?'

'Must be round the back,' said Burden. 'There wasn't room to build a garage on the side.'

They followed the drive round the back of the cottage. It led them to an asbestos hut with a felt roof, a building which couldn't be seen from the lane.

'If she went for a drive,' said Wexford, 'and brought someone back with her, the chances are they got the car into this garage without a soul seeing them. They'd have gone into the house by the kitchen door. We'll be lucky if we find anyone who saw them.'

In silence they regarded the moonlit empty fields that mounted towards wooded hills. Here and there, in the distance, an occasional light twinkled. And as they walked back towards the road, they were aware of how isolated the house was, how secluded the lane. Its high banks, crowned by massive overhanging trees, made it a black tunnel by night, a sylvan unfrequented corridor by day.

'The nearest house,' said Wexford, 'is that place up by the Stowerton Road, and the only other one is Wool Farm. That's a good half-mile down there.' He pointed through the tree tunnel and then he went off to his car. 'We can say goodbye to our weekend,' he said. 'See you first thing in the morning.'

The chief inspector's own home was to the north of Kingsmarkham on the other side of the Kingsbrook. His bedroom light was on and his wife still awake when he let himself in. Dora Wexford was too placid and too sensible to wait up for her husband, but she had been baby-sitting for her elder daughter and had only just got back. He found her sitting up in bed reading, a glass of hot milk beside her, and although he had only parted from her four hours before, he went up to her and kissed her warmly. The kiss was warmer than usual because, happy as his marriage was, contented with his lot as he was, it sometimes took external disaster to bring home to him his good fortune and how much he valued his wife. Another man's wife was dead, had died foully … He pushed aside squeamishness, his small-hours sensitivity and, starting to undress, asked Dora what she knew of the occupants of Bury Cottage.

'Where's Bury Cottage?'

'In Wool Lane. A man called Hathall lives there. His wife was strangled this afternoon.'

Thirty years of marriage to a policeman hadn't blunted Dora Wexford's sensibilities or coarsened her speech or made her untender, but it was only natural that she could no longer react to such a statement with the average woman's horror.

'Oh, dear,' she said, and conventionally, 'How dreadful! Is it going to be straightforward?'

'Don't know yet.' Her soft calm voice steadied him as it always did. 'Have you ever come across these people?'

'The only person I've ever come across in Wool Lane is that Mrs Lake. She came to the Women's Institute a couple of times, but I think she was too busy in other directions to bother much with that. Very much a one for the men, you know.'

'You don't mean the Women's Institute black-balled her?' said Wexford in mock-horror.

'Don't be so silly, darling. We're not narrow-minded. She's a widow, after all. I can't think why she hasn't married again.'

'Maybe she's like George the Second.'

'Not a bit. She's very pretty. What *do* you mean?'

'He promised his wife on her death-bed that he wouldn't marry again but only take mistresses.' While Dora giggled, Wexford studied his figure in the glass, drawing in the muscles of his belly. In the past year he had lost three stone in weight, thanks to diet, exercise and the terror inspired in him by his doctor, and for the first time in a decade he could regard his own reflection with contentment if not with actual delight. Now he could feel that it had been worth it. The agony of going without everything he liked to eat and drink had been worth while. *Il faut souffrir pour être beau.* If only there was something one could go without, some strenuous game one could play, that would result in remedying hair loss ...

'Come to bed,' said Dora. 'If you don't stop preening yourself, I'll think you're going to take mistresses, and I'm not dead yet.'

Wexford grinned and got into bed. Quite early in his career he had taught himself not to dwell on work during the night, and work had seldom kept him awake or troubled his dreams. But as he switched off the bed lamp and cuddled up to Dora – so much easier and pleasanter now he was thin – he allowed himself a few minutes' reflection on the events of the evening. It could be a straightforward case, it very well could be. Angela Hathall had been young and probably nice to look at. She was childless, and though house-proud, must have found time hanging heavily on her hands during those lonely weekdays and lonely nights. What more likely than that she had picked up some man and brought him back to Bury Cottage? Wexford knew that a woman need not be desperate or a nymphomaniac or on the road to prostitution to do this. She need not even intend infidelity. For women's attitudes to sex, whatever the new thought may hold, are not the same as men's. And though it is broadly true that a man who will pick up an unknown woman is only 'after one thing' and broadly speaking she knows it, she will cling to the generous belief that he wants nothing but conversation and perhaps a kiss. Had this been Angela Hathall's belief? Had she picked up a man in her car, a man who wanted more than that and had strangled her because he couldn't get it? Had he killed her and left her on the bed and then made a getaway in her car?

It could be. Wexford decided he would work along these lines. Turning his thoughts to more pleasant topics, his grandchildren, his recent holiday, he was soon asleep.

3

'Mr Hathall,' Wexford said, 'you no doubt have your own ideas as to how this sort of enquiry should be conducted. You will perhaps think my methods unorthodox, but they are my methods and I can assure you they get results. I can't conduct my investigation on circumstantial evidence alone. It's necessary for me to know as much as I can about the persons involved, so if you can answer my questions simply and realistically we shall get on a lot faster. I can assure you I shall ask them from the pure and direct motive of wanting to discover who killed your wife. If you take offence we shall be delayed. If you insist that certain matters concern only your private life and refuse to disclose them, a good deal of precious time may be lost. Do you understand that and will you be co-operative?'

This speech had been occasioned by Hathall's reaction to the first query that Wexford had put to him at nine on the Saturday morning. It had been a simple request for information as to whether Angela had been in the habit of giving lifts to strangers, but Hathall, who seemed refreshed by his night of drugged sleep, had flared at it in a burst of ill-temper.

'What right have you got to impugn my wife's moral character?'

Wexford had said quietly, 'The great majority of people who give lifts to hitch-hikers have no thought in their minds beyond that of being helpful,' and then, when Hathall continued to stare at him with bitter angry eyes, he had delivered his lecture.

The widower made an impatient gesture, shrugging and throwing out his hands. 'In a case like this I should have thought you'd go on fingerprints and – well, that sort of thing. I mean, it's obvious some man got in here and ... He must have left traces. I've read about how these things are conducted. It's a question of deduction from hairs and footmarks and – well, fingerprints.'

'I've already said I'm sure you have your own ideas as to how an enquiry should be conducted. My methods include those you have put forward. You saw for yourself how thoroughly this house was gone over last night, but we're not magicians, Mr Hathall. We can't find a fingerprint or a hair at midnight and tell you whose it is nine hours later.'

'When will you be able to?'

'That I can't say. Certainly by later today I should have some idea as to whether a stranger entered Bury Cottage yesterday afternoon.'

'A *stranger*? Of course it was a stranger. I could have told you that myself at eight o'clock last night. A pathological killer who got in here, broke in, I daresay, and – and afterwards stole my car. Have you found my car yet?'

Very smoothly and coldly, Wexford said, 'I don't know, Mr Hathall. I am not God, nor have I second sight. I haven't yet even had time to contact my officers. If you'll answer the one question I've put to you, I'll leave you for a while and go and talk to your mother.'

'My mother knows nothing whatever about it. My mother never set foot in this house till last night.'

'My question, Mr Hathall.'

'No, she wasn't in the habit of giving lifts,' Hathall shouted, his face crimson and distorted. 'She was too shy and nervous even to make friends down here. I was the only person she could trust, and no wonder after what she'd been through. The man who got in here knew that, he knew she was always alone. You want to work on that, get to work on that one. That's my private life, as you call it. I'd only been married three years and I worshipped my wife. But I left her alone all week because I couldn't face the journey up and down and this is what it's come to. She was scared stiff of being alone here. I said it wouldn't be for much longer and to stick it for my sake. Well, it wasn't for much longer, was it?'

He threw his arm over the back of the chair and buried his face in the crook of his elbow, his body shaking. Wexford watched him thoughtfully but said no more. He made his way towards the kitchen where he found Mrs Hathall at the sink, washing breakfast dishes. There was a pair of rubber gloves on the counter but they were dry and Mrs Hathall's bare hands were immersed in the suds. She was the sort of woman, he decided, who would be masochistic about housework, would probably use a brush rather than a vacuum cleaner and aver that washing machines didn't get clothes clean. He saw that instead of an apron she wore a checked tea towel tied round her waist, and this struck him as strange. Obviously she wouldn't have brought an apron with her for a weekend visit, but surely anyone as houseproud as Angela would have possessed several? However, he made no comment on it, but said good morning and asked Mrs Hathall if she would mind answering a few questions while she worked.

'Hmm,' said Mrs Hathall. She rinsed her hands and turned round slowly to dry them on a towel which hung from a rack. 'It's no good asking me. I don't know what she got up to while he was away.'

'I understand your daughter-in-law was shy and lonely, kept herself to herself, as you might say.' The noise she made fascinated him. It was part choke, part grunt, with a hint of the death rattle. He assumed it was, in fact, a laugh. 'She didn't impress you in that way?'

'Erotic,' said Mrs Hathall.

'I beg your pardon?'

24

She looked at him with scorn. 'Nervy. More like hysterical.'

'Ah,' said Wexford. This particular malapropism was new to him and he savoured it. 'Why was that, I wonder? Why was she – er, neurotic?'

'I couldn't say. I only saw her once.'

But they had been married for three years ... 'I'm not sure I understand, Mrs Hathall.'

She shifted her gaze from his face to the window, from the window to the sink, and then she picked up another cloth and began drying the dishes. Her solid board of a body, its back turned to him, was as expressive of discouragement and exclusion as a closed door. She dried every cup and glass and plate and piece of cutlery in silence, scoured the draining board, dried it, hung the cloth up with the concentration of one practising an intricate and hard-learned skill. But at last she was obliged to turn again and confront his seated patient figure.

'I've got the beds to make,' she said.

'Your daughter-in-law has been murdered, Mrs Hathall.'

'I ought to know that. I found her.'

'Yes. How was that exactly?'

'I've already said. I've told it all already.' She opened the broom cupboard, took a brush, a duster, superfluous tools unneeded in that speckless house. 'I've got work to do, if you haven't.'

'Mrs Hathall,' he said softly, 'do you realize that you will have to appear at the inquest? You're a most important witness. You will be very closely questioned and you will *not be able* to refuse to answer then. I can understand that you have never before come into contact with the law, but I must tell you that there are serious penalties attached to obstructing the police.'

She stared at him sullenly, only a little awed. 'I should never have come here,' she muttered. 'I said I'd never set foot here and I should have stuck to it.'

'Why did you come?'

'Because my son insisted. He wanted things patched up.' She plodded to within a yard of him and stopped. Wexford was reminded of an illustration in a storybook belonging to one of his grandsons, a picture of a cabinet with arms and legs and a surly face. 'I'll tell you one thing,' she said. 'If that Angela was nervy, it was shame that did it. She was ashamed of breaking up his marriage and making him a poor man. And so she should have been, she ruined three people's lives. I'll say that at your inquest. I don't mind telling anyone that.'

'I doubt,' said Wexford, 'if you will be asked. I'm asking you about last night.'

She jerked up her head. Petulantly, she said, 'I'm sure I've nothing to hide. I'm thinking of him, having everything dragged out in the open. She was supposed to meet us at the station last night.' A dry 'Hmm' snapped off the last word.

'But she was dead, Mrs Hathall.'

Ignoring him, she went on shortly and rapidly, 'We got here and he went to look for her. He called out to her. He looked everywhere downstairs and in the garden and in the garage.'

'And upstairs?'

'He didn't go upstairs. He told me to go upstairs and take my things off. I went in their bedroom and there she was. Satisfied? Ask him and see if he can tell you different.' The walking cupboard stumped out of the room and the stairs creaked as it mounted them.

Wexford went back into the room where Hathall was, not moving stealthily but not making much noise either. He had been in the kitchen for about half an hour, and perhaps Hathall believed he had already left the house, for he had made a very rapid recovery from his abandonment to grief, and was standing by the window peering closely at something on the front page of the morning paper. The expression on his lean ruddy face was one of extreme concentration, intense, even calculating, and his hands were quite steady. Wexford gave a slight cough. Hathall didn't jump. He turned round and the anguish which Wexford could have sworn was real again convulsed his face.

'I won't bother you again now, Mr Hathall. I've been thinking about this and I believe it would be much better for you to talk to me in different surroundings. Under the circumstances, these aren't perhaps the best for the sort of talk we must have. Will you come down to the police station at about three, please, and ask for me?'

Hathall nodded. He seemed relieved. 'I'm sorry I lost my temper just now.'

'That's all right. It was natural. Before you come this afternoon, would you have a look through your wife's things and tell me if you think anything is missing?'

'Yes, I'll do that. Your men won't want to go over the place any more?'

'No, all that's over.'

As soon as Wexford reached his own office in Kingsmarkham police station, he looked through the morning papers and found the one Hathall had been scrutinizing, the *Daily Telegraph*. At the foot of the front page, in the stop press, was a paragraph about an inch deep which read: 'Mrs Angela Hathall, 32, was last night found dead at her home in Wool Lane, Kingsmarkham, Sussex. She had been strangled. Police are treating the case as murder.' It was this on which Hathall's eyes had been fixed with such intensity. Wexford pondered for a moment. If his wife had been found murdered, the last thing he would have wanted would be to read about it in the paper. He spoke this thought aloud as Burden came into the room, adding that it didn't do to project one's own feelings on to others, for we can't all be the same.

'Sometimes,' said Burden rather gloomily, 'I think that if everyone was like you and me the world would be a better place.'

'Arrogant devil, you are. Have we got anything from the fingerprint boys yet? Hathall's dead keen on prints. He's one of those people who labour under the misapprehension that we're like foxhounds. Show us a print or a footmark and we put our noses to the ground and follow spoor until we run down our quarry about two hours later.'

Burden snorted. He thrust a sheaf of papers under the chief inspector's nose. 'It's all here,' he said. 'I've had a look and there are points of interest, but the fox isn't going to turn up in two hours or anything like it. Whoever he is, he's far, far away, and you can tell John Peel that one.'

Grinning, Wexford said, 'No sign of that car, I suppose?'

'It'll probably turn up in Glasgow or somewhere in the middle of next week. Martin checked with that company of Hathall's, Marcus Flower. He had a word with his secretary. She's called Linda Kipling and she says Hathall was there all day yesterday. They both came in at about ten – my God, I should be so lucky! – and apart from an hour and a half off for lunch, Hathall was there till he left at five-thirty.'

'Just because I said he'd been reading about his wife's murder in the paper, I didn't mean I thought he'd done it, you know.' Wexford patted the seat of the chair next to his own and said, 'Sit down Mike, and tell me what's in that – that ream you've brought me. Condense it. I'll have a look at it myself later.'

The inspector sat down and put on his newly acquired glasses. They were elegant glasses with narrow black frames and they gave Burden the look of a successful barrister. With his large collection of well-tailored suits, his expertly cut fair hair and a figure that needed no dieting to keep it trim, he had never had the air of a detective – a fact which had been to his advantage. His voice was prim and precise, a little more self-conscious than usual, because he wasn't yet accustomed to the glasses which he seemed to regard as changing his whole appearance and indeed his personality.

'The first thing to note, I'd say,' he began, 'is that there weren't nearly as many prints about the house as one would expect. It was an exceptionally well-kept house, everything very clean and well polished. She must have cleaned it very thoroughly indeed because there were hardly any of Hathall's own prints. There was a clear whole handprint on the front door and prints on other doors and the banisters, but those were obviously made after he got home last night. Mrs Hathall senior's prints were on the kitchen counter, the banisters, in the back bedroom, on the bathroom taps and lavatory cistern, on the telephone and, oddly enough, on the picture rail on the landing.'

'Not oddly enough at all,' said Wexford. 'She's the sort of old battleaxe who'd feel along a picture rail to see if her daughter-in-law had dusted it. And if she hadn't, she'd probably write "slut" or something equally provocative in the dust.'

Burden adjusted his glasses, smudged them with his fingertip and rubbed impatiently at them with his shirt cuff. 'Angela's prints were on the back door, the door from the kitchen into the hall, her bedroom door and on various bottles and jars on her dressing table. But they weren't anywhere else. Apparently she wore gloves for doing her housework, and if she took off her gloves to go to the bathroom, she wiped everything afterwards.'

'Sounds bloody obsessional to me. But I suppose some women do go on like that.'

Burden, whose expression conveyed that he rather approved of women who went on like that, said, 'The only other prints in the house were those of one unknown man and one unknown woman. The man's were found only on books and on the inside of a bedroom cupboard door, not Angela's bedroom. There's one single print of this other woman. It too was a whole handprint, the right hand, very clear, showing a small L-shaped scar on the forefinger, and it was found on the edge of the bath.'

'Hmm,' said Wexford, and because the sound reminded him of Mrs Hathall, he changed it to 'Huh'. He paused thoughtfully. 'I don't suppose these prints are on record?'

'Don't know yet. Give them time.'

'No, I mustn't be like Hathall. Is there anything else?'

'Some coarse long dark hairs, three of them, on the bathroom floor. They're not Angela's. Hers were finer. Hers alone were in her hairbrush on the dressing table.'

'Man's or woman's?'

'Impossible to tell. You know how long some blokes wear their hair these days.' Burden touched his own sleek crop and took off his glasses. 'We shan't get anything from the postmortem till tonight.'

'OK. We have to find that car and we have to find someone who saw her go out in it and, let's hope, someone who saw her and her pick-up come back in it – if that's the way it was. We have to find her friends. She must have had *some* friends.'

They went down in the lift and crossed the black and white checkerboard foyer. While Burden paused for a word with the station sergeant, Wexford went up to the swing doors that gave on to the steps and the courtyard. A woman was coming up those steps, walking confidently in the manner of one who has never known rejection. Wexford held the right-hand door open for her, and as she came face to face with him she stopped and looked him full in the eyes.

She wasn't young. Her age couldn't have been far short of fifty, but it was at once apparent that she was one of those rare creatures whom time cannot wither or stale or devitalize. Every fine line on her face seemed the mark of laughter and mischievous wit, but there were few of these around her large bright blue and surprisingly young eyes. She smiled at him, a smile to make a man's heart turn over, and said:

'Good morning. My name is Nancy Lake. I want to see a policeman, the top one, someone very important. Are you important?'

'I daresay I will do,' said Wexford.

She looked him over as no woman had looked him over for twenty years. The smile became musing, delicate eyebrows went up. 'I really think you might,' she said, and stepping inside, 'However, we must be serious. I've come to tell you I think I was the last person to see Angela Hathall alive.'

4

When a pretty woman ages, a man's reaction is usually to reflect on how lovely she must once have been. This was not Nancy Lake's effect. There was something very much of the here and now about her. When with her you thought no more of her youth and her coming old age than you think of spring or Christmas when you are enjoying late summer. She was of the season in which they were, a harvest-time woman, who brought to mind grape festivals and ripened fruit and long warm nights. These thoughts came to Wexford much later. As he led her into his office, he was aware only of how extremely pleasing this diversion was in the midst of murder and recalcitrant witnesses and fingerprints and missing cars. Besides, it wasn't exactly a diversion.

Happy is the man who can combine pleasure and business ...

'What a nice room,' she said. Her voice was low and sweet and lively. 'I thought police stations were brown and murky with photographs on the walls of great brutes all wanted for robbing banks.' She glanced with warm approval at his carpet, his yellow chairs, his rosewood desk. 'This is lovely. And what a nice view over all those delicious little roofs. May I sit down?'

Wexford was already holding the chair for her. He was recalling what Dora had said about this woman being 'very much for the men' and added to this statement one of his own: that the men would be very much for her. She was dark. Her hair was abundant and of a rich chestnut brown, probably dyed. But her skin had kept a rose and amber glow, the texture of a peach, and a delicate light seemed to shine from beneath its surface as is sometimes seen in the faces of young girls or children, but which is rarely retained into middle age. The red lips seemed always on the edge of a smile. It was as if she knew some delightful secret which she would almost, but never wholly, divulge. Her dress was just what, in Wexford's opinion, a woman's dress should be, full in the skirt, tight in the waist, of mauve and blue printed cotton, its low neck showing an inch or two of the upper slopes of a full golden bosom. She saw that he was studying her and she seemed to enjoy his scrutiny, basking in it, understanding more thoroughly than he himself what it meant.

He shifted his gaze abruptly. 'You live in the

house at the Kingsmarkham end of Wool Lane, I believe?'

'It's called Sunnybank. I always think that sounds like a mental hospital. But my late husband chose the name and I expect he had his reasons.'

Wexford made a determined and eventually successful attempt to look grave. 'Were you a friend of Mrs Hathall's?'

'Oh, *no*.' He thought she was capable of saying she had no women friends, which would have displeased him, but she didn't. 'I only went there for the miracles.'

'The *what*?'

'An in-joke. I'm sorry. I meant the yellow egg plums.'

'Ah, mira*belles*.' This was the second malapropism of his day, but he decided this particular instance was a deliberate mistake. 'You went there yesterday to pick plums?'

'I always do. Every year. I used to when old Mr Somerset lived there, and when the Hathalls came they said I could have them. I make them into jam.'

He had a sudden vision of Nancy Lake standing in a sunfilled kitchen, stirring a pot full of the golden fruit. He smelt the scent of it, saw her face as she dipped in a finger and brought it to those full red lips. The vision threatened to develop into a fantasy. He shook it off. 'When did you go there?'

The roughness in his voice made her eyebrows go up. 'I phoned Angela at nine in the morning and asked if I could go up there and pick them. I'd noticed they were falling. She seemed quite pleased – for her. She wasn't a very gracious person, you know.'

'I don't know. I hope you'll tell me.'

She moved her hands a little deprecatingly, casually. 'She said to come about half past twelve. I picked the plums and she gave me a cup of coffee. I think she only asked me in to show me how nice the house looked.'

'Why? Didn't it always look nice?'

'Goodness, no. Not that I care, that was her business. I'm not much for housework myself, but Angela's house was usually a bit of a pigsty. Anyway, it was a mess last March which was when I was last in it. She told me she'd cleaned it up to impress Robert's mother.'

Wexford nodded. He had to make an effort of will to continue questioning her in this impersonal way, for she exercised a spell, the magical combination of feminine niceness and strong sexuality. But the effort had to be made. 'Did she tell you she was expecting another caller, Mrs Lake?'

'No, she said she was going out in the car, but she didn't say where.' Nancy Lake leant across the desk rather earnestly, bringing her face to within a foot of his. Her perfume was fruity and warm. 'She asked me in and gave me coffee, but as soon as I'd had one cup she seemed to want to get rid of me. That's what I meant by saying she only wanted to show me how nice the house looked.'

'What time did you leave?'

'Let me see. It would have been just before half

past one. But I was only in the house ten minutes. The rest of the time I was picking the miracles.'

The temptation to remain close to that vital, mobile and somehow mischievous face was great, but it had to be resisted. Wexford swivelled his chair round with deliberate casualness, turning to Nancy Lake a stern and businesslike profile. 'You didn't see her leave Bury Cottage or return to it later?'

'No, I went to Myringham. I was in Myringham the whole afternoon and part of the evening.'

For the first time there was something guarded and secretive in her reply, but he made no comment. 'Tell me about Angela Hathall. What sort of person was she?'

'Brusque, tough, ungracious.' She shrugged, as if such failings in woman were beyond her comprehension. 'Perhaps that's why she and Robert got on so well together.'

'Did they? They were a happy couple?'

'Oh, very. They had no eyes for anyone else, as the saying is.' Nancy Lake gave a light laugh. 'All in all to each other, you know. They had no friends, as far as I could tell.'

'I've been given the impression she was shy and nervous.'

'Have you now? I wouldn't say that. I got the idea she was on her own so much because she liked it that way. Of course, they'd been very badly off till he got this new job. She told me they only had fifteen pounds a week to live on after all his outgoings. He was paying alimony or whatever it's called to his first wife.' She paused and smiled.

'People make such messes of their lives, don't they?'

There was a hint of ruefulness in her voice as if she had experience of such messes. He turned round again, for a thought had struck him. 'May I see your right hand, Mrs Lake?'

She gave it to him without question, not laying it on the table but placing it palm-downwards in his. It was almost a lover-like gesture and one that has become typical of the beginning of a relationship between a man and a woman, this covering of hand by hand, a first approach, a show of comfort and trust. Wexford felt its warmth, observed how smooth and tended it was, noted the soft sheen of the nails and the diamond ring which encircled the middle finger. Bemused, he let it rest there a fraction too long.

'If anyone had told me,' she said, her eyes dancing, 'that I should be holding hands with a policeman this morning, I shouldn't have believed them.'

Wexford said stiffly, 'I beg your pardon,' and turned her hand over. No L-shaped scar marred the smooth surface of the tip of her forefinger, and he let the hand drop.

'Is that how you check fingerprints? Goodness, I always thought it was a much more complicated process.'

'It is.' He didn't explain. 'Did Angela Hathall have a woman in to help with the cleaning?'

'Not as far as I know. They couldn't have afforded it.' She was doing her best to conceal her delight at his discomfiture, but he saw her lips twitch and delight won. 'Can I be of any further service to you, Mr Wexford? You wouldn't care to make casts of my footprints, for instance, or take a blood sample?'

'No, thank you. That won't be necessary. But I may want to talk to you again, Mrs Lake.'

'I do hope you will.' She got up gracefully and took a few steps towards the window. Wexford, who was obliged to rise when she did, found himself standing close beside her. She had manoeuvred this, he knew she had, but he could only feel flattered. How many years was it since a woman had flirted with him, had wanted to be with him and enjoyed the touch of his hand? Dora had done so, of course, his wife had done so … As he was drawing himself up, conscious of his new firm figure, he remembered his wife. He remembered that he was not only a policeman but a husband who must be mindful of his marriage vows. But Nancy Lake had laid her hand lightly on his arm, was drawing his attention to the sunshine outside, the cars in the High Street that had begun their long progress to the coast.

'Just the weather for a day by the sea, isn't it?' she said. The remark sounded wistful, like an invitation. 'What a shame you have to work on a Saturday.' What a shame work and convention and prudence prevented him from leading this woman to his car, driving her to some quiet hotel. Champagne and roses, he thought, and that hand once more reaching across a table to lie warmly in his … 'And the winter will soon be here,' she said.

Surely she couldn't have meant it, couldn't have intended that double meaning? That the winter would soon be there for both of them, the flesh falling, the blood growing cold ... 'I mustn't keep you,' he said, his voice as icy as that coming winter.

She laughed, not at all offended, but she took her hand from his arm and walked towards the door. 'You might at least say it was good of me to come.'

'It was. Very public-spirited. Good morning, Mrs Lake.'

'Good morning, Mr Wexford. You must come to tea quite soon and I'll give you some miracle jam.'

He sent for someone to see her out. Instead of sitting down once more behind his desk, he returned to the window and looked down. And there she was, crossing the courtyard with the assurance of youth, as if the world belonged to her. It didn't occur to him that she would look back and up but she did, suddenly, as if his thoughts had communicated themselves to her and called that swift glance. She waved. Her arm went up straight and she waved her hand. They might have known each other all their lives, so warm and free and intimate was that gesture, having separated after a delightful assignation that was no less sweet because it was customary. He raised his own arm in something like a salute, and then, when she had disappeared among the crowd of Saturday shoppers, he too went down to find Burden and take him off for lunch.

The Carousel Café, opposite the police station, was always crowded at Saturday lunchtime, but at least the juke box was silent. The real noise would start when the kids came in at six. Burden was sitting at the corner table they kept permanently reserved, and when Wexford approached, the proprietor, a meek Italian, came up to him deferentially and with considerable respect.

'My special today for you, Chief Inspector. The liver and bacon I can recommend.'

'All right, Antonio, but none of your reconstituted potato, eh? And no monosodium glutamate.'

Antonio looked puzzled. 'This is not on my menu, Mr Wexford.'

'No, but it's there all right, the secret agent, the alimentary fifth column. I trust you've had no more speedy goings-on of late?'

'Thanks to you, sir, we have not.'

The reference was to an act of mischief performed a couple of weeks before by one of Antonio's youthful part-time employees. Bored by the sobriety of the clientele, this boy had introduced into the glass tank of orange juice with its floating plastic oranges, one hundred amphetamine tablets, and the result had been a merry near-riot, a hitherto decorous businessman actually dancing on a table top. Wexford, chancing to call in and, on account of his diet, sampling the orange juice himself, had located the source of this almost Saturnalian jollity and, simultaneously, the joker. Recalling all this now, he laughed heartily.

'What's so funny?' said Burden sourly. 'Or has that Mrs Lake been cheering you up?' When Wexford stopped laughing but didn't answer, he said, 'Martin's taken a room in the church hall, a sort of enquiry post and general information pool. The public are being notified in the hope that anyone who may have seen Angela on Friday afternoon will come in and tell us about it. And if she didn't go out, there's a possibility her visitor was seen.'

'She went out,' said Wexford. 'She told Mrs Lake she was going out in the car. I wonder who the lady with the L-shaped scar is, Mike. Not Mrs Lake, and Mrs Lake says Angela didn't have a cleaner or, come to that, any friends.'

'And who's the man who fingers the inside of cupboard doors?'

The arrival of the liver and bacon and Burden's spaghetti Bolognese silenced them for a few minutes. Wexford drank his orange juice, wistfully thinking how much he would enjoy it if this tankful had been 'speeded' up and Burden were suddenly to become merry and uninhibited. But the inspector, eating fastidiously, wore the resigned look of one who has sacrificed his weekend to duty. Deep lines, stretching from nostrils to the corners of his mouth, intensified as he said:

'I was going to take my kids to the seaside.'

Wexford thought of Nancy Lake who would look well in a swimsuit, but he switched off the picture before it developed into a full-colour three-dimensional image. 'Mike, at this stage of a case we usually ask each other if we've noticed anything odd, any discrepancies or downright untruths. Have you noticed anything?'

'Can't say I have, except the lack of prints.'

'She'd spring-cleaned the place to impress the old woman, though I agree it was strange she seems to have wiped everything again before going off on her car jaunt. Mrs Lake had coffee with her at about one, but Mrs Lake's prints aren't anywhere. But there's something else that strikes me as even odder than that, the way Hathall behaved when he got into the house last night.'

Burden pushed away his empty plate, contemplated the menu, and rejecting the idea of a sweet, signalled to Antonio for coffee. 'Was it odd?' he said.

'Hathall and his wife had been married for three years. During that time the old woman had only met her daughter-in-law once, and there had evidently been considerable antagonism between them. This appears to have been something to do with Angela's having broken up Hathall's first marriage. Be that as it may – and I mean to learn more about it – Angela and her mother-in-law seem to have been at loggerheads. Yet there was a kind of *rapprochement*, the old woman had been persuaded to come for the weekend and Angela was preparing to receive her to the extent of titivating the place far beyond her normal standard. Now Angela was supposed to be meeting them at the station, but she didn't turn up. Hathall says she was shy and nervous, Mrs Lake that she was brusque and ungracious. Bearing this in mind, what conclusions would you expect Hathall to have drawn when his wife wasn't at the station?'

'That she'd got cold feet. That she was too frightened to face her mother-in-law.'

'Exactly. But what happened when he got to Bury Cottage? He couldn't find Angela. He looked for her *downstairs* and in the garden. He never went upstairs at all. And yet by then he must have suspected Angela's nervousness and concluded surely that a nervous woman takes refuge not in the garden but in her own bedroom. But instead of looking upstairs for her, *he sent his mother*, the very person he must have believed Angela to be frightened of. This shy and nervous girl to whom he is alleged to be devoted was cowering – he must have thought – in her bedroom, but instead of going up to reassure her and then bring her to confront his mother with him there to support her, he goes off to the garage. That, Mike, is very odd indeed.'

Burden nodded. 'Drink your coffee,' he said. 'You said Hathall was coming in at three. Maybe he'll give you an answer.'

5

Although Wexford pretended to study the list of missing articles – a bracelet, a couple of rings and a gilt neck chain – Hathall had brought him, he was really observing the man himself. He had come into the office with head bowed, and now he sat silent, his hands folded in his lap. But the combination of ruddy skin and black hair gives a man an angry look. Hathall, in spite of his grief, looked angry and resentful. His hard craggy features had the appearance of being carved out of roseate granite, his hands were large and red, and even his eyes, though not bloodshot, held a red gleam. Wexford wouldn't have judged him attractive to women, yet he had had two wives. Was it perhaps that certain women, very feminine or nervous or maladjusted women, saw him as a rock to which they might cling, a stronghold where they might find shelter? Possibly that colouring of his indicated passion and tenacity and strength as well as ill-temper.

Wexford placed the list on his desk and, looking up, said, 'What do you think happened yesterday afternoon, Mr Hathall?'

'Are you asking *me* that?'

'Presumably you knew your wife better than anyone else knew her. You'd know who would be likely to call on her or be fetched home by her.'

Hathall frowned, and the frown darkened his whole face. 'I've already said, some man got into the house for the purpose of robbery. He took those things on that list and when my wife interrupted him, he – he killed her. What else could it have been? It's obvious.'

'I don't think so. I believe that whoever came to your house wiped the place clean of a considerable number of fingerprints. A thief wouldn't have needed to do that. He'd have worn gloves. And although he might have struck your wife, he wouldn't have strangled her. Besides, I see here that you value the missing property at less than fifty pounds all told. True, people have been killed for less, but I doubt if any woman has ever been strangled for such a reason.'

When Wexford repeated the word 'strangled', Hathall again bowed his head. 'What alternative is there?' he muttered.

'Tell me who came to your house. What friends or acquaintances called on your wife?'

'We had no friends,' said Hathall. 'When we came here we were more or less on the breadline. You need money to make friends in a place like this. We hadn't got the money to join clubs or give dinner parties or even have people in for drinks. Angela often didn't see a soul from Sunday night till Friday night. And the friends I'd had before I married her – well, my first wife saw to it I'd lost them.' He coughed impatiently and tossed his head in the way his mother had. 'Look, I think I'd better tell you a bit about what Angela and I had been through, and then perhaps you'll see that all this talk of friends calling is arrant nonsense.'

'Perhaps you had, Mr Hathall.'

'It'll be my life history.' Hathall gave a humourless bark of laughter. It was the bitter laugh of the paranoiac. 'I started off as an office boy with a firm of accountants, Craig and Butler, of Gray's Inn Road. Later on, when I was a clerk there, the senior partner wanted me to be articled and persuaded me to study for the Institute's exams. In the meantime I'd got married and I was buying a house in Croydon on a mortgage, so the extra money was handy.' He looked up with another aggrieved frown. 'I don't think there's ever been a time till now when I've had a reasonable amount of money to live on, and now I've got it it's no good to me.

'My first marriage wasn't happy. My mother may think it was but outsiders don't know. I got married seventeen years ago and two years later I knew I'd made a mistake. But we'd got a daughter by that time, so there wasn't anything I could do about it. I expect I'd have jogged along and made the best of it if I hadn't met Angela at an office party. When I fell in love with her and knew that – well, what I felt for her was returned, I asked my wife for a divorce. Eileen – that's my first wife's name – made hideous scenes. She brought my mother into it and she even brought Rosemary in – a kid of eleven. I can't describe what my life was like and I won't try to.'

'This was five years ago?'

'About five years ago, yes. Eventually I left home and went to live with Angela. She had a room in Earls Court and she was working at the library of the National Archaeologists' League.' Hathall, who had said he couldn't describe what his life had been like, immediately proceeded to do so. 'Eileen set about a – a campaign of persecution. She made scenes at my office and at Angela's place of work. She even came to Earls Court. I begged her for a divorce. Angela had a good job and I was doing all right. I thought I could have afforded it, whatever demands Eileen made. In the end she agreed, but by that time Butler had sacked me on account of Eileen's scenes, sacked me out of hand. It was a piece of outrageous injustice. And, to crown it all, Angela had to leave the library. She was on the verge of a nervous breakdown.

'I got a part-time job as accountant with a firm of toy manufacturers, Kidd and Co., of Toxborough, and Angela and I got a room nearby. We were on our beam ends. Angela couldn't work. The divorce judge awarded Eileen my house and custody of my daughter and a very unfairly large slice out of my very inadequate income. Then we had what looked like a piece of luck at last. Angela has a cousin down here, a man called Mark Somerset, who let us have Bury Cottage. It had been his father's, but of course there wasn't any question of its being rent-free – he didn't take his generosity that far, in spite of being a blood relation. And I can't say he ever did anything else for us. He didn't even befriend Angela, though he must have known how lonely she was.

'Things went on like this for nearly three years. We were literally living on about fifteen pounds a week. I was still paying off the mortgage on a house I haven't set foot in for four years. My mother and my first wife had poisoned my daughter's mind against me. What's the use of a judge giving you reasonable access to a child if the child refuses to come near you? I remember you said you'd want to know about my private life. Well, that was it. Nothing but harassment and persecution. Angela was the one bright spot in it and now – and now she's dead.'

Wexford, who believed that, with certain exceptions, a man only suffers chronic and acute persecution if something masochistic in his psychological make-up seeks persecution, pursed his lips. 'This man Somerset, did he ever come to Bury Cottage?'

'Never. He showed us over the place when he first offered it to us, and after that, apart from a chance meeting in the street in Myringham, we never saw him again. It was as if he'd taken an unreasonable dislike to Angela.'

So many people had disliked or resented her. She

sounded, Wexford thought, as inclined to paranoia as her husband. Generally speaking, nice people are not much disliked. And a kind of widespread conspiracy of hatred against them, which Hathall seemed to infer, is never feasible.

'You say this was an unreasonable dislike, Mr Hathall. Was your mother's dislike equally unreasonable?'

'My mother is devoted to Eileen. She's old-fashioned and rigid and she was prejudiced against Angela for what she calls her taking me away from Eileen. It's complete nonsense to say that a woman can steal another woman's husband if he doesn't want to be – well, stolen.'

'They only met once, I believe. Was that meeting not a success?'

'I persuaded my mother to come to Earls Court and meet Angela. I should have known better, but I thought that when she actually got to know her she might get over the feeling she was a kind of scarlet woman. My mother took exception to Angela's clothes – she was wearing those jeans and that red shirt – and when she said something uncomplimentary about Eileen my mother walked straight out of the house.'

Hathall's face had grown even redder at the memory. Wexford said, 'So they weren't on speaking terms for the whole of your second marriage?'

'My mother refused to visit us or have us come to her. She saw me, of course. I tell you frankly, I'd have liked to cut myself off from her entirely but I felt I had a duty towards her.'

Wexford always took such assertions of virtue with a grain of salt. He couldn't help wondering if old Mrs Hathall, who must have been nearly seventy, had some savings to leave.

'What brought about the idea of the reunion you planned for this weekend?'

'When I landed this job with Marcus Flower – at, incidentally, double the salary I'd been getting from Kidd's – I decided to spend my week nights at my mother's place. She lives in Balham, so it wasn't too far for me to go into Victoria. Angela and I were looking for a flat to buy in London, so it wouldn't have gone on for too long. But, as usual with me, disaster hit me. However, as I was saying, I'd spent every week night at my mother's since July and I'd had a chance to talk to her about Angela and how much I'd like them to be on good terms. It took eight weeks of persuasion, but she did at last agree to come here for a weekend. Angela was very nervous at the whole idea. Of course she was as anxious for my mother to like her as I was, but she was very apprehensive. She scrubbed the whole place from top to bottom so that my mother couldn't find any fault there. I shall never know now whether it would have worked out.'

'Now, Mr Hathall, when you got to the station last night and your wife wasn't there to meet you as had been arranged, what was your reaction?'

'I don't follow you,' said Hathall shortly.

'What did you feel? Alarmed? Annoyed? Or just disappointed?'

Hathall hesitated. 'I certainly wasn't annoyed,'

he said. 'I suppose I thought it was an unfortunate start to the weekend. I assumed Angela had been too nervous to come, after all.'

'I see. And when you reached the house, what did you do?'

'I don't know what all this is leading up to, but I suppose there's some purpose behind it.' Again Hathall gave that impatient toss of the head. 'I called out to Angela. When she didn't answer, I looked for her in the dining room and in the kitchen. She wasn't there, so I went out into the garden. Then I told my mother to go upstairs while I looked to see if the car was in the garage.'

'You thought perhaps that you on foot and your wife in the car might have missed each other?'

'I don't know what I thought. I just naturally looked everywhere for her.'

'But not upstairs, Mr Hathall?' said Wexford quietly.

'Not at first. I would have done.'

'Wasn't it likely that of all places in the house a nervous woman, afraid to meet her mother-in-law, would have been, the first was her own bedroom? But you didn't go there first, as might have been expected. You went to the garage and sent your mother upstairs.'

Hathall, who might have blustered, who might have told Wexford to state plainly what he was getting at, said instead in a rather stiff and awkward tone, 'We can't always account for our actions.'

'I disagree. I think we can if we look honestly into our motives.'

'Well, I suppose I thought if she hadn't answered my call, she couldn't be in the house. Yes, I did think that. I thought she must have set off in the car and we'd missed each other because she'd gone some other way round.'

But some other way round would have meant driving a mile down Wool Lane to its junction with the Pomfret to Myringham road, then following this road to Pomfret or Stowerton before doubling back to Kingsmarkham station, a journey of five miles at least instead of a half-mile trip. But Wexford said no more about it. Another factor in the man's behaviour had suddenly struck him, and he wanted to be alone to think about it, to work out whether it was significant or merely the result of a quirk in his character.

As Hathall rose to go, he said, 'May I ask you something now?'

'By all means.'

But Hathall seemed to hesitate, as if still to postpone some burning question or to conceal it under another of less moment. 'Have you had anything from the – well, the pathologist yet?'

'Not yet, Mr Hathall.'

The red rock face tightened. 'These fingerprints. Have you got something from them yet? Isn't there some clue there?'

'Very little, as far as we can tell.'

'It seems a slow process to me. But I know nothing about it. You'll keep me informed, will you?'

He had spoken hectoringly, like a company chairman addressing a junior executive. 'Once an arrest has been made,' said Wexford, 'you may be sure you won't be left in the dark.'

'That's all very well, but neither will any newspaper reader. I should like to know about this ...' He bit off the sentence as if he had been tending towards an end it might have been unwise to approach. 'I should like to know about this pathologist's report.'

'I will call on you tomorrow, Mr Hathall,' said Wexford. 'In the meantime, try to keep calm and rest as much as you can.'

Hathall left the office, bowing his head as he went. Wexford couldn't escape the notion that he had bowed it to impress the young detective constable who had shown him out. Yet the man's grief seemed real. But grief, as Wexford knew, is much easier to simulate than happiness. It demands little more than a subdued voice, the occasional outburst of righteous anger, the reiteration of one's pain. A man like Hathall, who believed the world owed him a living and who suffered from a persecution complex, would have no difficulty in intensifying his normal attitude.

But why had he shown no sign of shock? Why, above all, had he never shown that stunned disbelief which is the first characteristic reaction of one whose wife or husband or child has met with a violent death? Wexford thought back over the three conversations he had had with Hathall, but he wasn't able to recall a single instance of disbelief in awful reality. And he recalled similar situations, bereaved husbands who had interrupted his questions with cries that it couldn't be true, widows who had exclaimed that it couldn't be happening to them, that it was a dream from which they must soon awaken. Disbelief temporarily crowds out grief. Sometimes whole days pass before the fact can be realized, let alone accepted. Hathall had realized and accepted at once. It seemed to Wexford, as he sat musing and awaiting the postmortem results, that he had accepted even before he let himself in at his own front door.

'So she was strangled with a gilt necklace,' said Burden. 'It must have been a pretty tough one.'

Looking up from the report, Wexford said, 'It could be the one on Hathall's list. It says here a gilt ligature. Some shreds of gilding were found embedded in her skin. No tissue from her killer found under her fingernails, so there was presumably no struggle. Time of death, between one-thirty and three-thirty. Well, we know it wasn't one-thirty because that was when Mrs Lake left her. She seems to have been a healthy woman, she wasn't pregnant, and there was no sexual assault.' He gave Burden a condensed version of what Robert Hathall had told him. 'The whole thing's beginning to look peculiar now, isn't it?'

'You mean you've got it into your head that Hathall had some sort of guilty knowledge?'

'I know he didn't kill her. He couldn't have done. When she died he was at this Marcus Flower place with Linda Whatsit and God knows how many other people. And I don't see any motive there. He seems to have been fond of her, if no one else was.

But why didn't he go upstairs last night, why isn't he stunned with shock, and why does he get so worked-up about fingerprints?'

'The killer must have hung around after the deed was done to wipe off prints, you know. He must have touched things in the bedroom and the other rooms, and then forgotten what he *had* touched, so that he had to do a big clean-up job to be on the safe side. Otherwise Angela's and Mrs Lake's prints would have been in the living room. Doesn't that argue a lack of premeditation?'

'Probably. And I think you're right. I don't for a moment believe Angela was so fanatical or so frightened of her mother-in-law that she polished the living room after Mrs Lake had gone as well as before she came.'

'It's a funny thing, though, that he went to all that trouble, yet still left prints on the inside of a door to a cupboard in a spare room, a cupboard that was apparently never used.'

'If he did, Mike,' said Wexford, 'if he did. I think we're going to find that those prints belong to a Mr Mark Somerset, the owner of Bury Cottage. We'll find out just where in Myringham he lives and then we'd better get over to see him.'

6

Myringham, where the University of the South is situated, lies about fifteen miles from Kingsmarkham. It boasts a museum, a motte and bailey castle and one of the best-preserved remains of a Roman villa in Britain. And although a new centre has grown up between the university buildings and the railway station, a place of tower blocks and shopping precincts and multi-storey car parks, all this red brick and concrete has been kept well away from the old town which stands, unspoilt, on the banks of the Kingsbrook.

Here there are narrow lanes and winding by-streets that call to the mind of the visitor the paintings of Jacob Vrel. The houses are very old, some – of brown brick and worm-eaten grey-brown timber

– built before the Wars of the Roses, or even, it is said, before Agincourt. Not all of them have owner-occupiers or steady tenants, for some have fallen into such disrepair, such dismal decay, that their owners cannot afford to put them in order. Squatters have taken possession of them, secure in their ancient right from police interference, safe from eviction because their 'landlords' are prevented by law from demolishing their property and by lack of money from repairing it.

But these form only a small colony of the Old Town. Mark Somerset lived in the smarter part, in one of the old houses by the river. In the days when England was Catholic it had been a priest's house and in one of the walls of its garden was a narrow and beautiful stained-glass window, for this was also a wall of St Luke's Church. The Myringham Catholics had a new church now in the new town, and the presbytery was a modern house. But here where the brown walls clustered about the church and the mill, the fifteenth century still lingered.

There was nothing fifteenth century about Mark Somerset. An athletic-looking man in his fifties, he wore neat black jeans and a tee-shirt, and Wexford detected his age only by the lines about his bright blue eyes and the veining of his strong hands. The man's belly was flat, his chest well muscled, and he had the good fortune to keep his hair which, having once been golden, was now silver-gilt.

'Ah, the fuzz,' he said, his smile and pleasant tone robbing the greeting of rudeness. 'I thought you'd turn up.'

'Shouldn't we have turned up, Mr Somerset?'

'Don't know. That's for you to decide. Come in, but be as quiet as you can in the hall, will you? My wife only came out of hospital this morning and she's just managed to get off to sleep.'

'Nothing serious, I hope?' said Burden fatuously – and unnecessarily, in Wexford's view.

Somerset smiled. It was a smile of sad experience, of endurance, tinged very slightly with contempt. He spoke in a near-whisper. 'She's been an invalid for years. But you haven't come to talk about that. Shall we go in here?'

The room had a beamed ceiling and panelled walls. A pair of glass doors, a later but pleasing addition, were open to a small paved garden backed by the riverside trees, and the foliage of these trees looked like black lace against the amber flare of the setting sun. Beside these doors was a low table on which was a bottle of hock in an ice-bucket.

'I'm a sports coach at the university,' said Somerset. 'Saturday night's the only time I allow myself a drink. Will you have some wine?'

The two policemen accepted and Somerset fetched three glasses from a cabinet. The Liebfraumilch had the delicate quality peculiar to some kinds of hock, that of tasting like liquid flowers. It was ice-cold, scented, dry.

'This is very kind of you, Mr Somerset,' said Wexford. 'You're disarming me. I hardly like to ask you now if we may take your fingerprints.'

Somerset laughed. 'You can take my fingerprints with pleasure. I suppose you've found the prints of some unknown mystery man at Bury Cottage, have you? They're probably mine, though I haven't been in the place for three years. They can't be my father's. I had the whole place redecorated after he died.' He spread out his strong work-broadened hands with a kind of bold innocence.

'I understand you didn't get on with your cousin?'

'Well, now,' said Somerset, 'rather than let you interrogate me and probably put to me a lot of time-wasting questions, wouldn't it be better if I told you what I know about my cousin and gave you a sort of history of our relationship? Then you can ask me what you like afterwards.'

Wexford said, 'That's exactly what we want.'

'Good.' Somerset had the good teacher's succinct crisp manner. 'You wouldn't want me to have any squeamishness about not speaking ill of the dead, would you? Not that I have much ill to speak of Angela. I was sorry for her. I thought she was feeble, and I don't much care for feeble people. I first met her about five years ago. She'd come to this country from Australia and I'd never seen her before. But she was my cousin all right, the daughter of my father's dead brother, so you needn't get any ideas she might have been an impostor.'

'You have been reading too many detective stories, Mr Somerset.'

'Maybe.' Somerset grinned and went on, 'She looked me up because I and my father were the only relatives she had in this country, and she was lonely in London. Or so she said. I think she was on the look-out for any pickings there might be for her. She was a greedy girl, poor Angela. She hadn't met Robert at that time. When she did she stopped coming out here and I didn't hear from her again until they were about to get married and hadn't anywhere to live. I'd written to her to tell her of my father's death – to which, by the way, she didn't reply – and she wanted to know if I'd let her and Robert have Bury Cottage.

'Well, I'd been meaning to sell it, but I couldn't get the price I wanted, so I agreed and let it to Angela and Robert for five pounds a week.'

'A very low rent, Mr Somerset,' said Wexford, interrupting him. 'You could have got at least twice that.'

Somerset shrugged. Without asking them he refilled their glasses. 'Apparently, they were very badly off, and she was my cousin. I have some silly old-fashioned ideas about blood being thicker than water, Mr Wexford, and I can't shake them off. I didn't in the least mind letting them have the place furnished at what was little more than a nominal rent. What I did mind was when Angela sent me her electricity bill for me to pay.'

'You'd made no agreement about that, of course?'

'Of course not. I asked her to come over here and we'd talk about it. Well, she came and spun me the old sob story I'd heard from her before about their poverty, her nerves and her unhappy adolescence with her mother who wouldn't let her go to university. I suggested that if money was so tight with them she should get a job. She was a qualified librarian and she could easily have got a library job at Kingsmarkham or Stowerton. She pleaded her mental breakdown, but she seemed perfectly healthy to me. I think she was just lazy. Anyway, she flounced out of the house, telling me I was mean, and I didn't see either her or Robert again until about eighteen months ago. On that occasion they didn't see me. I was out with a friend in Pomfret and I saw Robert and Angela through the windows of a restaurant. It was a very expensive restaurant and they seemed to be doing themselves proud, so I came to the conclusion they were doing a good deal better financially.

'We actually *met* again only once more. That was last April. We ran into each other in Myringham in that monstrosity the planners are pleased to call a shopping precinct. They were loaded down with stuff they'd bought, but they seemed depressed in spite of the fact that Robert had got himself this new job. Perhaps they were only embarrassed at coming face to face with me. I never saw Angela again. She wrote to me about a month ago to say that they'd want to leave the cottage as soon as they'd got a place in London, and that that would probably be in the New Year.'

'Were they a happy couple?' Burden asked when Somerset had finished.

'Very, as far as I could tell.' Somerset got up to close the glass doors as the sunset light faded and a little wind rose. 'They had so much in common. Should I be very mean-spirited if I said that what they had in common were paranoia, greed and a general idea that the world owed them a living? I'm sorry she's dead, I'm sorry to hear of anyone dying like that, but I can't say I liked her. Men can be gauche and tough as they please, but I like a little grace in a woman, don't you? I don't want to be fanciful, but I sometimes thought Robert and Angela got on so well because they were united in gracelessness against the world.'

'You've been very helpful, Mr Somerset,' said Wexford more as a matter of form than with sincerity. Somerset had told him much he didn't know, but had he told him anything that mattered? 'You won't take it amiss, I'm sure, if I ask you what you were doing yesterday afternoon.'

He could have sworn the man hesitated. It was as if he had already thought up how he must answer, but still had to brace himself to give that answer. 'I was here alone. I took the afternoon off to get things ready for my wife's coming home. I'm afraid I was quite alone and I didn't see anyone, so I can't give you confirmation.'

'Very well,' said Wexford. 'That can't be helped. I don't suppose you have any idea as to what friends your cousin had?'

'None at all. According to her, she had no friends. Everyone she'd ever known but Robert had been cruel to her, she said, so making friends was just to invite more cruelty.' Somerset drained his glass. 'Have some more wine?'

'No, thank you. We've taken enough of your Saturday-night ration as it is.'

Somerset gave them his pleasant frank smile. I'll see you to the door.'

As they came out into the hall, a querulous voice sounded from upstairs: 'Marky, Marky, where are you?'

Somerset winced, perhaps only at the ugly diminutive. But blood is thicker than water, and a man and his wife are one. He went to the foot of the stairs, called out that he was just coming, and opened the front door. Wexford and Burden said good night quickly, for the voice from above had risen to a thin petulant wail.

In the morning Wexford returned as he had promised to Bury Cottage. He had news, some of which had only just reached him, for Robert Hathall, but he had no intention of telling the widower what he most wanted to know.

Mrs Hathall let him in and said her son was still asleep. She showed him into the living room and told him to wait there, but she offered him neither tea nor coffee. She was the kind of woman, he decided, who had probably seldom if ever in her life dispensed refreshment to anyone but members of her own family. They were a strange guarded lot, these Hathalls, whose isolationism apparently infected the people they married, for when he asked Mrs Hathall if Angela's predecessor had ever been to the cottage, she said:

'Eileen wouldn't have lowered herself. She keeps herself to herself.'

'And Rosemary, your grand-daughter?'

'Rosemary came once, and once was enough. Anyway, she's too busy with her schoolwork to go out and about.'

'Will you give me Mrs Eileen Hathall's address, please?'

Mrs Hathall's face grew as red as her son's, as red as the wrinkled skin on a turkey's neck. 'No, I won't! You've no business with Eileen. Find it out for yourself.' She banged the door on him and he was left alone.

It was the first time he had ever been alone there, so he used the waiting time to survey the room. The furniture, which he had supposed to be Angela's and had therefore credited her with taste, was in fact Somerset's, the lifelong collection perhaps of Somerset's father. It was the prettiest kind of late-Victorian with some earlier pieces, spindle-legged chairs, an elegant small oval table. By the window was a red and white Venetian glass oil-lamp that had never been converted to electricity. A glass-fronted bookcase contained, for the most part, the kind of works an old man would have collected and loved: a complete set of Kipling bound in red leather, some H.G. Wells, Gosse's *Father and Son*, a little of Ruskin and a lot of Trollope. But on the top shelf, where previously perhaps had stood an ornament, were the Hathalls' own books. There were half a dozen thrillers in paperback, two or three works of 'pop' archaeology, a couple of novels which had aroused controversy over their sexual content when they had been published, and two handsomely jacketed imposing tomes.

Wexford took down the first of these. It was a volume of colour prints of ancient Egyptian jewellery, contained scarcely any text apart from the captions beneath the pictures, and bore inside its front cover a plate which proclaimed it as the property of the library of the National Archaeologists' League. Stolen, of course, by Angela. But books, like umbrellas, pens and boxes of matches, belong in a category of objects the stealing of which is a very venial offence, and Wexford thought little of it. He replaced the book and took out the last one on the shelf. Its title was *Of Men and Angels, A Study of Ancient British Tongues*, and when he opened it he saw that it was a very learned work with chapters on the origins of Welsh, Erse, Scottish Gaelic and Cornish and their common Celtic source. Its price was nearly six pounds, and he wondered that anyone as poor as the Hathalls had claimed to have been should have spent so much on something which was surely as far above their heads as it was above his own.

He was still holding the book when Hathall came into the room. He saw the man's eyes go warily to it, then look sharply away.

'I didn't know you were a student of Celtic languages, Mr Hathall,' he said pleasantly.

'It was Angela's. I don't know where it came from, but she'd had it for ages.'

'Strange, since it was only published this year. But no matter. I thought you'd like to know that your car has been found. It had been abandoned in London, in a side street near Wood Green station. Are you familiar with the district?'

66

'I've never been there.' Hathall's gaze kept returning, with a kind of reluctant fascination or perhaps apprehensively, to the book Wexford still kept hold of. And for this very reason Wexford determined to keep hold of it and not to remove the finger which he had slipped at random between its pages as if to keep a place. 'When can I have it back?'

'In two or three days. When we've had a good look at it.'

'Examined it for those famous fingerprints you're always on about, I suppose?'

'Am I, Mr Hathall? I? Aren't you rather projecting on to me what you think I ought to feel?' Wexford looked blandly at him. No, he wouldn't gratify the man's curiosity, though it was hard to tell now what Hathall most longed for. A revelation of what the fingerprints had disclosed? Or for that book to be laid down casually as of no account? 'My present feeling is that you should stop worrying about investigations which only we can make. Your mind may be eased a little when I tell you your wife hadn't been sexually assaulted.' He waited for some sign of relief, but only saw those eyes with their red glint dart once more to the book. And there was no response when he said as he prepared to leave, 'Your wife died very quickly, in perhaps no more than fifteen seconds. It's possible that she scarcely knew what was happening to her.'

Getting up, he eased his finger from the pages of the book and slipped the jacket flap in where it had been. 'You won't mind if I borrow this for a few days, will you?' he said, and Hathall shrugged but still said nothing at all.

7

The inquest took place on Tuesday morning, and a verdict was returned of murder by person or persons unknown. Afterwards, as Wexford was crossing the courtyard between the coroner's court and the police station, he saw Nancy Lake go up to Robert Hathall and his mother. She began to speak to Hathall, to condole with him perhaps or offer him a lift home to Wool Lane in her car. Hathall snapped something short and sharp at her, took his mother's arm and walked off rapidly, leaving Nancy standing there, one hand up to her lips. Wexford watched this little pantomime, which had taken place out of earshot, and was nearing the car-park exit when a car drew up alongside him and a sweet vibrant voice said:

'Are you very very busy, Chief Inspector?'

'Why do you ask, Mrs Lake?'

'Not because I have any fascinating clues to give you.' She put her hand out of the window and beckoned to him. It was a mischievous and seductive gesture. He found it irresistible and he went up to her and bent down. 'The fact is,' she said, 'that I have a table for two booked at the Peacock in Pomfret and my escort has most churlishly stood me up. Would you think it very forward of me if I asked you to lunch with me instead?'

He was staggered. There was no doubt now that this rich, pretty and entirely charming woman was making advances to him – *him*! It was forward all right, it was almost unprecedented. She looked at him calmly, the corners of her mouth tilted, her eyes shining.

But it wouldn't do. Along whatever paths of fantasy his imagination might lead him, into whatever picture galleries of erotica, it wouldn't do. Once though, when he was young and without ties or prestige or pressures, it could have been a different story. And in those days he had taken such offers or made them without much appreciation and with little awareness of their delight. Ah, to be a little bit younger and know what one knows now …!

'But I also have a table booked for lunch,' he said, 'at the Carousel Café.'

'You won't cancel that and be my guest?'

'Mrs Lake, I am, as you said, very very busy. Would you think *me* forward if I said you would distract me from my business?'

She laughed, but it wasn't a laugh of merriment,

and her eyes had ceased to dance. 'It's something, I suppose, to be a distraction,' she said. 'You make me wonder if I've ever been anything but a – distraction. Good-bye.'

He went quickly away and up in the lift to his office, wondering if he had been a fool, if such a chance would ever come to him again. He attached no special significance to her words, neither to ponder on them nor to try and interpret them, for he couldn't think of her intellectually. In his mind, her face went with him, so seductive, so hopeful, then so downcast because he had refused her invitation. He tried to thrust this image away and concentrate on what was before him, the dry and technical report on the examination of Robert Hathall's car, but it kept returning, and with it her entrancing voice, reduced now to a cajoling whisper.

Not that there was much in the report to get excited about. The car had been found parked in a street near Alexandra Park, and the discovery had been made by a constable on the beat. It was empty but for a couple of maps and a ball-point pen on the dashboard shelf, and inside and out it had been wiped clean. The only prints were those of Robert Hathall, found on the underside of the boot and bonnet lids, and the only hairs two of Angela's on the driving seat.

He sent for Sergeant Martin, but got nothing encouraging from him. No one claiming to be a friend of Angela's had come forward, and nobody, apparently, had seen her go out or return home on Friday afternoon. Burden was out, making enquiries

– for the second or third time – among the workers at Wool Farm, so Wexford went alone to the Carousel Café for a solitary lunch.

It was early, not much past midday, and the café was still half-empty. He had been sitting at his corner table for perhaps five minutes and had ordered Antonio's speciality of the day, roast lamb, when he felt a light touch that was almost a caress on his shoulder. Wexford had had too many shocks in his life to jump. He turned round slowly and said with a cool note in his voice that he didn't feel, 'This is an unexpected pleasure.'

Nancy Lake sat down opposite him. She made the place look squalid. Her cream silk suit, her chestnut silk hair, her diamonds and her smile threw into sordid relief Antonio's Woolworth cutlery and the tomato-shaped plastic sauce container.

'The mountain,' she said, 'wouldn't come to Mahomet.'

He grinned. It was pointless to pretend he wasn't delighted to see her. 'Ah, you should have seen me a year ago,' he said. 'Then I *was* a mountain. What will you eat? The roast lamb will be bad, but better than the pie.'

'I don't want to eat anything. I'll just have coffee. Aren't you flattered that I didn't come for the food?'

He was. Eyeing the heaped plate which Antonio set before him, he said, 'It's not much of a compliment, though. Coffee only for the lady, please.' Were her attractions enhanced, he asked himself, by Antonio's obvious admiration of them? She was aware of it all, he could see that, and in her awareness, her experienced acceptance of her powers, lay one of the few signs of her age.

She was silent for a few moments while he ate, and he noticed that her expression was one of rueful repose. But suddenly, as he was preparing to ask her why Robert Hathall had repulsed her so violently that morning, she looked up and said:

'I'm sad, Mr Wexford. Things aren't going well for me.'

He was very surprised. 'Do you want to tell me about it?' How strange that their intimacy had advanced so far that he could ask her that ...

'I don't know,' she said. 'No, I don't think so. One gets conditioned into habits of secrecy and discretion, even if one doesn't personally see much point in them.'

'That's true. Or can be true in certain circumstances.' The circumstances Dora had referred to?

Yet she was on the brink of telling him. Perhaps it was only the arrival of her coffee and Antonio's admiring flutterings that deterred her. She gave a little shrug, but instead of the small-talk that he expected, she said something that astonished him. It was so surprising and so intensely spoken that he pushed away his plate and stared at her.

'Is it very wrong, d'you think, to want someone to die?'

'Not,' he said, puzzled, 'if that wish remains just a wish. Most of us wish that sometimes, and most of us, fortunately, let I dare not wait upon I would.'

'Like the poor cat in the adage?'

He was delighted that she had capped his quotation. 'Is this – er, enemy of yours connected with these habits of secrecy and discretion?'

She nodded. 'But I shouldn't have brought it up. It was silly of me. I'm very lucky really, only it gets hard sometimes, alternating between being a queen and a – distraction. I shall get my crown back, this year, next year, sometime. I shall never abdicate. Goodness, all this mystery! And you're much too clever not to have guessed what I'm on about, aren't you?' He didn't reply to that one. 'Let's change the subject,' she said.

So they changed the subject. Afterwards, when she had left him and he found himself standing, bemused, in the High Street, he could hardly have said what they had talked about, only that it had been pleasant, too pleasant, and had left him with most unpleasant feelings of guilt. But he would see her no more. If necessary, he would eat his lunch in the police canteen, he would avoid her, he would never again be alone with her, even in a restaurant. It was as if he had committed adultery, had confessed it, and been told to 'avoid the occasion'. But he had committed nothing, not even himself. He had only talked and listened.

Had what he had listened to helped him? Perhaps. All that circumlocution, those hints at an enemy, at secrecy and discretion, that had been a pointer. Hathall, he knew, would admit nothing, would have had his ego boosted by the coroner's sympathy. Yet, knowing all this, he nevertheless set off along the

High Street towards Wool Lane. He had no idea that it was to be his last visit to Bury Cottage, and that, although he would see Hathall again, it was to be more than a year before they exchanged another word.

Wexford had forgotten all about the book of Celtic languages, hadn't, in fact, bothered to glance at it again, but it was with a request for its immediate return that Hathall greeted him.

'I'll have it sent over to you tomorrow,' he said.

Hathall looked relieved. 'There's also the matter of my car. I need my car.'

'You can have that tomorrow as well.'

The sour old woman was evidently in the kitchen, closeted behind a shut door. She had maintained the house in the immaculate condition in which her dead daughter-in-law had left it, but the touch of an alien and tasteless hand was already apparent. On old Mr Somerset's oval table stood a vase of plastic flowers. What impulse, festive or funereal, had prompted Mrs Hathall to buy them and place them there? *Plastic* flowers, thought Wexford, in the season of mellow fruitfulness when real flowers filled the gardens and the hedgerows and the florists' shops.

Hathall didn't ask him to sit down and he didn't sit down himself. He stood with one elbow resting on the mantelpiece, his fist pressed into his hard red cheek.

'So you didn't find anything incriminating in my car?'

'I didn't say that, Mr Hathall.'

'Well, did you?'

'As a matter of fact, no. Whoever killed your wife was very clever. I don't know that I've ever come across anyone in this sort of situation who covered his tracks so expertly.' Wexford piled it on, letting a note of grudging admiration creep into his voice. Hathall listened impassively. And if gratified was too strong a word to use to describe his expression, satisfied wasn't. The fist uncurled and relaxed, and he leant back against the fireplace with something like arrogance. 'He seems to have worn gloves to drive your car,' Wexford said, 'and to have given it a wash as well, for good measure. Apparently, he wasn't seen to park the car, and no one was seen driving it on Friday. At the moment, we really have very few leads to go on.'

'Will – will you find any more?' He was eager to know, but as anxious to disguise his eagerness.

'It's early days yet, Mr Hathall. Who knows?' Perhaps it was cruel to play with the man. Does the end ever justify the means? And Wexford didn't know what end he was aiming for, or where next to grab in this game of hide-and-seek in a dark room. 'I can tell you that we found the fingerprints of a man, other than your own, in this house.'

'Are they on – what d'you call it? – record?'

'They proved to be those of Mr Mark Somerset.'

'Ah, well …' Suddenly Hathall looked more genial than Wexford had ever seen him. Perhaps only an inhibition as to touching prevented him from stepping forward to pat the chief inspector on the back. 'I'm sorry,' he said. 'I'm not myself at the moment. I should have asked you to sit down. So the only prints you found were those of Mr Somerset, were they? Dear Cousin Mark, our tight-fisted landlord.'

'I didn't say that, Mr Hathall.'

'Well, and mine and – and Angela's, of course.'

'Of course. But apart from those, we found a whole handprint of a woman in your bathroom. It's the print of her right hand, and on the tip of the forefinger is an L-shaped scar.'

Wexford had expected a reaction. But he believed Hathall to be so well under control that he had thought that reaction would show itself only as fresh indignation. He would expostulate perhaps, ask why the police hadn't followed this evidence up, or with a shrug of impatience suggest that this was the handprint of some friend of his wife's whose existence, in his grief, he had forgotten to mention. Never had he supposed, feeling his way in the dark as he was, that his words would have had such a cataclysmic effect.

For Hathall froze where he stood. Life seemed driven out of him. It was as if he had suddenly been stricken with a pain so great that it had paralysed him or forced him to hold himself still for the protection of his heart and his whole nervous system. And yet he said nothing, he made no sound. His self-control *was* magnificent. But his body, his physical self, was triumphing over his mental processes. It was as strong an example of matter over mind as Wexford had ever seen. The shock had come to Hathall at last. The stunning, with its attendant disbelief and terror and realization of what the future must now be, which should have bludgeoned him when he first saw his wife's body, was taking effect five days later. He was pole-axed by it.

Wexford was excited but he behaved very casually. 'Perhaps you can throw some light on whose this handprint may be?'

Hathall drew in his breath. He seemed to have a very real need of oxygen. Slowly he shook his head.

'No idea at all, Mr Hathall?'

The head-shaking went on. It was robot-like, automatic, as if running on some dreadful cerebral clockwork, and Wexford had the notion that Hathall would have to take his head in both hands and grasp it to stop that slow mechanical movement.

'A clear handprint on the side of your bath. An L-shaped scar on the right forefinger. We shall, of course, take it as a lead for our main line of enquiry.'

Hathall jerked up his chin. A spasm ran through his body. He forced a thin constricted voice through stiff lips. 'On the bath, you said?'

'On the bath. I'm right, aren't I, in thinking you can guess whose it may be?'

'I haven't,' Hathall said tremulously and weakly, 'the faintest idea.' His skin had taken on a mottled pallor, but now the blood returned to it and pulsed in the veins on his forehead. The worst of the shock was over. It had been replaced by – what? Not anger, not indignation. Sorrow,

Wexford thought, surprised. He was overcome at this late stage by real sorrow …

Wexford felt no impulse to be merciful. He said relentlessly, 'I've noticed how anxious you've been right through my enquiries to know what we've deduced from fingerprints. In fact, I've never known a bereaved husband to take quite such a keen interest in forensics. Therefore, I can't help feeling you expected a certain print to be found. If that's so and we've found it, I must tell you that you'll be obstructing this enquiry if you keep what may be vital information to yourself.'

'Don't threaten me!' Though the words were sharp, the voice that spoke them was feeble and the huffiness in the tone pathetically assumed. 'Don't think you can persecute me.'

'I should rather advise *you* to think over what I've said, and then, if you are wise, you'll make a frank disclosure to us of what I'm sure you know.'

But even as he spoke, looking into the man's miserable, shocked eyes, he knew that any such disclosure would be far from wise. For whatever alibi the man might have, whatever love for her and devotion to her he might profess, he had killed his wife. And as he left the room, making his own way out of the house, he imagined Robert Hathall collapsing into a chair, breathing shallowly, feeling his racing heart, gathering his resources for very survival.

The revelation that they had found a woman's handprint had done this to him. Therefore, he knew who that woman was. He had been anxious about fingerprints because all the time he had dreaded she might have left this evidence behind. But his reaction hadn't been that of a man who merely suspects something or fears the confirmation of a fact he has guessed at. It had been the reaction of someone who fears for his own liberty and peace, the liberty and peace too of another, and, above all, that he and that other might not now have that liberty and peace together.

8

His discovery had driven from Wexford's mind memories of that lunchtime interlude. But when he walked into his own house soon after four they returned to him, discoloured by guilt. And if he hadn't spent that hour in Nancy Lake's company, or if it had been less enjoyable, he might not now have given Dora such a hearty kiss or asked her what he did ask her.

'How would you like to go up to London for a couple of days?'

'You mean you have to go?'

Wexford nodded.

'And you can't bear to be parted from me?' Wexford felt himself blushing. Why did she have to be so perceptive? It was almost as if she read his thoughts. But if she had been less perceptive, would he have married her? 'I'd love to, darling,' she said blandly. 'When?'

'If Howard and Denise will have us, as soon as you can pack a bag.' He grinned, knowing the quantity of clothes she would want to take with her for even two days with his fashionable niece. 'Like – ten minutes?'

'Give me an hour,' said Dora.

'OK. I'll phone Denise.'

Chief Superintendent Howard Fortune, the head of Kenbourne Vale CID, was the son of Wexford's dead sister. For years Wexford had been in awe of him, his awe mixed with envy of this nephew, so aptly named, into whose lap so many good things had fallen, apparently without effort on his part, a first-class honours degree, a house in Chelsea, marriage to a beautiful fashion model, rapid promotion until his rank far surpassed his uncle's. And these two had taken on in his eyes the hard gloss of jet-set people, entering, although he hardly knew them, into that category of rich relations who will despise us from a distance and snub us if we make overtures to them. With misgivings he had gone to stay with them to convalesce after an illness, and his misgivings had turned out to be groundless, the silly suspicions that are born only of a grudge. For Howard and Denise had been kind and hospitable and unassuming, and when he had helped Howard solve a Kenbourne Vale murder case – solved it himself, Howard said – he had felt he was vindicated and a friendship established.

Just how firm that friendship was to be had been shown by the Fortunes' enjoyment of family Christmases at Wexford's house, by the new *rapport* between uncle and nephew, and revealed itself again in the greeting the chief inspector and his wife got as their taxi brought them to the house in Teresa Street. It was just after seven and one of Denise's elaborate dinners was almost ready.

'But you've got so thin, Uncle Reg,' she said as she kissed him. 'Here was I, counting calories for you, and now it looks as if it was all labour in vain. You look quite handsome.'

'Thank you, my dear. I must confess my weight loss has removed one of my principal fears of London.'

'And what would that be?'

'That *was* that I'd get myself inside one of those automatic ticket things on the Underground – you know, the kind with the snapping jaws – and be unable to get out.'

Denise laughed and took them into the living room. Since that first visit, Wexford had got over his fear of knocking over Denise's flower arrangements and conquered his awe of her fragile china ornaments and the pastel satin upholstery he was sure he would ruin with coffee stains. The abundance of everything, the smooth-running splendours and the air of gracious living, no longer intimidated him. He could sit with ease on a chair in one of those little circles of chairs and a silk sofa that reminded him of photographs of royal palace interiors. He could laugh about the tropical central heating, or as now when it wasn't on, comment on its summer counterpart, the newly installed air conditioning.

'It reminds me,' he said, 'of that description of Scott's of the Lady Rowena's apartments. "The rich hangings shook to the night blast ... the flame of the torches streamed sideways into the air like the unfurled pennon of a chieftain." Only, in your case, it's house plants that stream and not flames.'

They had an in-joke about their exchange of quotations, for at one time Wexford had used them to assert his intellectual equality, and Howard had replied, or so his uncle believed, to keep discreetly off the subject of their shared occupation.

'Literary chit-chat, Reg?' said Howard, smiling.

'To break the ice only – and you'll get real ice on your flower vases if you keep that going, Denise. No, I want to talk to you about why I've come up here, but that'll keep till after dinner.'

'And I thought you'd come up here to see me!' said Denise.

'So I have, my dear, but another young woman is interesting me a good deal more at present.'

'What's she got that I haven't got?'

Wexford took her hand and, pretending to scrutinize it, said, 'An L-shaped scar on her forefinger.'

When Wexford was in London he always hoped people would take him for a Londoner. To sustain this illusion, he took certain measures such as remaining in his seat until the tube train had actually come to a halt at his destination instead of leaping up nervously thirty seconds beforehand as is the habit of non-Londoners. And he refrained from enquiring of other passengers if the train he was in was actually going to the place announced by the confusing indicator. As a result, he had once found himself in Uxbridge instead of Harrow-on-the-Hill. But there is no easy way of getting from the western reaches of Chelsea to the West End by Tube, so Wexford boarded the number 14 bus, an old friend.

Instead of one person, Marcus Flower turned out to be two, Jason Marcus and Stephen Flower, the former looking like a long-haired and youthful Ronald Colman and the latter a short-haired and superannuated Mick Jagger. Wexford refused a cup of the black coffee they were drinking – apparently as a hangover remedy – and said he had really come to talk to Linda Kipling. Marcus and Flower went off into a double act of innuendo at this, declaring that Miss Kipling was far better worth seeing than they, that no one ever came there except to look at the girls, and then, falling simultaneously grave, said almost in unison how frightfully sorry they had been to hear of 'poor old Bob's loss' about which they had been 'absolutely cut up'.

Wexford was then conducted by Marcus through a series of offices that were strangely lush and stark at the same time, rooms where the furniture was made of steel and leather and set against extravagant velvet drapes and high-pile carpets. On the walls were abstract paintings of the splashed ketchup and copulating spiders *genre*, and on low tables magazine pornography so soft as to be gently blancmange-like in texture and kind. The secretaries, three of them, were all together in a blue velvet room, the one who had received him, a red-headed one, and Linda Kipling. Two others, said Linda, were in one case at the hairdresser's and in the other at a wedding. It was that sort of place.

She led him into an empty office where she sat down on the kind of black leather and metal bench you find in airport lounges. She had the look of a dummy in the window of a very expensive dress shop, realistic but not real, as if made of high-quality plastic. Contemplating her fingernails, which were green, she told him that Robert Hathall had phoned his wife every day at lunchtime since he had been with them, either calling her himself or asking her to put the call through for him. This she had thought 'terribly sweet', though now, of course, it was 'terribly tragic'.

'You'd say he was very happily married, would you, Miss Kipling? Talked about his wife a lot, kept her photograph on his desk, that sort of thing?'

'He did have her photograph, but Liz said it was frightfully bourgeois, doing things like that, so he put it away. I wouldn't know if he was happy. He was never very *lively*, not like Jason and Steve and some of the other blokes.'

'What was he like last Friday?'

'The same as usual. *Just* the same. I've told that to a policeman already. I don't know what's the good of saying the same thing over and over again. He was just the same as usual. He got in a bit before ten and he was in here all the morning working out the details of a sort of scheme for private hospital treatment for those of the staff who wanted it. Insurance, you know.' Linda looked her contempt for those executives who couldn't afford to pay for their own private treatment. 'He phoned his wife a bit before one and then he went out to lunch in a pub with Jason. They weren't gone long. I know he was back here by half past two. He dictated three letters to me.' She seemed aggrieved at the memory, as if this had been an unfairly demanding task. 'And he went off at five-thirty to meet his mother and take her off to wherever he lives, somewhere in Sussex.'

'Did he ever get phone calls here from women or a woman?'

'His wife never phoned *him*.' His meaning sank in and she stared at him. She was one of those people who are so narrow and who have imaginations so limited that hints at anything unexpected in the field of sex or social conduct or the emotions throw them into fits of nervous giggles. She giggled now. 'A girlfriend, d'you mean? Nobody like that phoned him. No one ever phoned him.'

'Was he attracted by any of the girls here?'

She looked astonished and edged slightly away. 'The girls *here*?'

'Well, there are five girls here, Miss Kipling, and if the three of you I've seen are anything to go by, you're not exactly repulsive. Did Mr Hathall have a special friendship with any girl here?'

The green fingernails fluttered. 'Do you mean a relationship? D'you mean, was he *sleeping* with anyone?'

'If you like to put it that way. After all, he was a lonely man, temporarily separated from his wife. I suppose you were all here on Friday afternoon, none of you out having her hair done or at a wedding?'

'Of course we were all here! And as to Bob Hathall having a relationship with any of us, you might care to know that June and Liz are married, Clare's engaged to Jason and Suzanne is Lord Carthew's daughter.'

'Does that exempt her from sleeping with a man?'

'It exempts her from sleeping with someone of Bob Hathall's – er, kind. And that goes for all of us. We mayn't be "exactly repulsive", as you put it, but we haven't come down to that!'

Wexford said good morning to her and walked out, feeling rather sorry he had paid her even that one grudging compliment. In Piccadilly, he went into a call-box and dialled the number of Craig and Butler, Accountants, of Gray's Inn Road. Mr Butler, he was told, was at present engaged, but would be happy to see him at three o'clock that afternoon. How should he spend the intervening time? Although he had discovered Mrs Eileen Hathall's address, Croydon was too far distant to sandwich in a visit there between now and three. Why not find out a little more about Angela herself and get some background to this marriage that everyone said was happy but which had ended in murder? He leafed through the directory and found it: The National Archaeologists' League Library, 17 Trident Place,

Knightsbridge SW7. Briskly, he walked up to the Tube station in Piccadilly Circus.

Trident Place wasn't easy to find. Although he had consulted his *A to Z Guide* in the privacy of the call-box, he found he had to look at it again in full view of sophisticated Londoners. As he was telling himself he was an old fool to be so self-conscious, he was rewarded by the sight of Sloane Street from which, according to the guide, Trident Place debouched.

It was a wide street of four-storey mid-Victorian houses, all smart and well kept. Number seventeen had a pair of heavy glass doors, framed in mahogany, through which Wexford went into a hall hung with monochrome photographs of amphorae and with portraits of gloomy-looking unearthers of the past, and thence through another door into the library itself. The atmosphere was that of all such places, utterly quiet, scholarly, redolent of books, ancient and modern. There were very few people about. A member was busy with one of the huge leather-bound catalogues, another was signing for the books he had taken out. Two girls and a young man were occupied in a quiet and studious way behind the polished oak counter, and it was one of these girls who came out and took Wexford upstairs, past more portraits, more photographs, past the sepulchrally silent reading room, to the office of the chief librarian, Miss Marie Marcovitch.

Miss Marcovitch was a little elderly woman, presumably of Central European Jewish origin. She spoke fluent academic English with a slight accent. As unlike Linda Kipling as one woman can be unlike another, she asked him to sit down and showed no surprise that he had come to question her about a murder case, although she had not at first connected the girl who used to work for her with the dead woman.

'She left here, of course, before her marriage,' said Wexford. 'How would you describe her, as tough and ungracious, or nervous and shy?'

'Well, she was quiet. I could put it like this – but, no, the poor girl is dead.' After her small hesitation, Miss Marcovitch went on hastily, 'I really don't know what I can tell you about her. She was quite ordinary.'

'I should like you to tell me everything you know.'

'A tall order, even though she *was* ordinary. She came to work here about five years ago. It's not the usual practice of the library to employ people without university degrees, but Angela was a qualified librarian and she had some knowledge of archaeology. She'd no practical experience, but neither, for that matter, have I.'

The bookish atmosphere had reminded Wexford of a book he still had in his possession. 'Was she interested in Celtic languages?'

Miss Marcovitch looked surprised. 'Not that I know of.'

'Never mind. Please go on.'

'I hardly know how to go on, Chief Inspector. Angela did her work quite satisfactorily, though she was absent rather a lot on vague medical grounds. She was bad about money ...' Again Wexford noticed the hesitation. 'I mean, she couldn't manage on her salary and she used to complain that it was inadequate. I gathered she borrowed small sums from other members of the staff, but that was no business of mine.'

'I believed she worked here for some months before she met Mr Hathall?'

'I'm not at all sure when she did meet Mr Hathall. First of all she was friendly with a Mr Craig who used to be on our staff but who has since left. Indeed, all the members of our staff from that time have left except myself. I'm afraid I never met Mr Hathall.'

'But you did meet the first Mrs Hathall?'

The librarian pursed her lips and folded her small shrivelled hands in her lap. 'This seems very much like scandalmongering,' she said primly.

'So much of my work is, Miss Marcovitch.'

'Well ...' She gave a sudden unexpected smile, bright and almost naughty. 'In for a penny, in for a pound, eh? I did meet the first Mrs Hathall. I happened to be in the library itself when she came in. You'll have noticed that this is a very quiet place. Voices aren't raised and movements aren't swift, an atmosphere which suits members and staff alike. I must confess to having been very angry indeed when this woman burst into the library, rushed up to where Angela was behind the counter and began to rant and rave at her. It was impossible for members not to realize that she was reproaching Angela for what she called stealing her husband. I asked Mr Craig to get rid of the woman as quietly as he could, and then I took Angela upstairs with me. When she calmed down I told her that, although her private affairs were no business of mine, such a thing mustn't be allowed to occur again.'

'It didn't occur again?'

'No, but Angela's work began to suffer. She was the kind that goes to pieces easily under strain. I was sorry for her, but not otherwise sorry, when she said she'd have to give up her job on her doctor's advice.'

The librarian finished speaking, seemed to have said everything she had to say and was on her feet. But Wexford, instead of getting up, said in a dry voice, 'In for a pound, Miss Marcovitch?'

She coloured and gave a little embarrassed laugh. 'How perspicacious of you, Chief Inspector! Yes, there is one more thing. I suppose you noticed my hesitations. I've never told anyone about this, but – well, I will tell you.' She sat down again, and her manner became more pedantic. 'In view of the fact that the library members pay a large subscription – twenty-five pounds annually – and are by their nature careful of books, we charge no fines should they keep books beyond the allotted period of one month. Naturally, however, we don't publicize this, and many new members have been pleasantly surprised to find that, on returning books they have kept for perhaps two or three months, no charge is made.

'About three and a half years ago, a little while after Angela had left us, I happened to be helping out at the returns counter when a member handed to me three books that I saw were six weeks overdue.

I should have made no comment on this had the member not produced one pound eighty, which he assured me was the proper fine for overdue books, ten pence per week per book. When I told him no fines were ever exacted in this library, he said he'd only been a member for a year and had only once before kept books longer than a month. On that occasion the "young lady" had asked him for one pound twenty, and he hadn't protested, thinking it to be reasonable.

'Of course I made enquiries among the staff who all appeared perfectly innocent, but the two girls told me that other members had recently also tried to get them to accept fines for overdue books, which they had refused and had given an explanation of our rules.'

'You think Angela Hathall was responsible?' Wexford asked.

'Who else could have been? But she had gone, no very great harm was done, and I didn't relish raising this matter at a meeting of the trustees which might have led to trouble and perhaps to a prosecution with members called as witnesses and so on. Besides, the girl had been under a strain and it was a very small fraud. I doubt if she made more than ten pounds out of it at the most.'

9

A very small fraud ... Wexford hadn't expected to encounter fraud at all, and it was probably irrelevant. But the shadowy figure of Angela Hathall had now, like a shape looming out of fog, begun to take more definite outlines. A paranoid personality with a tendency to hypochondria; intelligent but unable to persevere at a steady job; her mental state easily overthrown by adversity; financially unstable and not above making extra money by fraudulent means. How, then, had she managed on the fifteen pounds a week which was all she and her husband had had to live on for a period of nearly three years?

He left the library and took the Tube to Chancery Lane. Craig and Butler, Accountants, had their offices on the third floor of an old building near the Royal Free Hospital. He noted the place, had a salad and orange juice lunch in a café, and at one minute to three was shown up into the office of the senior partner, William Butler. The room was as old-fashioned and nearly as quiet as the library, and Mr Butler as wizened as Miss Marcovitch. But he wore a jolly smile, the atmosphere was of business rather than scholarship, and the only portrait a highly coloured oil of an elderly man in evening dress.

'My former partner, Mr Craig,' said William Butler.

'It would be his son, I imagine, who introduced Robert and Angela Hathall?'

'His nephew. Paul Craig, the son, has been my partner since his father's retirement. It's Jonathan Craig who used to work at the archaeologists' place.'

'I believe the introduction took place at an office party here?'

The old man gave a sharp scratchy little chuckle. 'A party *here*? Where would we put the food and drink, not to mention the guests? They'd be reminded of their income tax and get gloomy and depressed. No, that party was at Mr Craig's own home in Finchley on his retirement from the firm after forty-five years.'

'You met Angela Hathall there?'

'It was the only time I did meet her. Nice-looking creature, though with a bit of that Shetland pony look so many of them have nowadays. Wearing trousers too. Personally, I think a woman should put on a skirt to go to a party. Bob Hathall was very smitten with her from the first, you could see that.'

'That can't have pleased Mr Jonathan Craig.'

Again Mr Butler gave his fiddle-string squawk. 'He wasn't serious about *her*. Got married since, as a matter of fact. His wife's nothing to look at but loaded, my dear fellow, pots of it. This Angela wouldn't have gone down at all well with the family, they're not easy-going like me. Mind you, even I took a bit of a dim view when she went up to Paul and said what a lovely job he'd got, just the thing for knowing how to fiddle one's tax. Saying that to an accountant's like telling a doctor he's lucky to be able to get hold of heroin.' And Mr Butler chortled merrily. 'I met the first Mrs Hathall too, you know,' he said. 'She was a lively one. We had quite a scene, what with her banging about trying to get to Bob, and Bob locking himself up in his office. What a voice she's got when she's roused! Another time she sat on the stairs all day waiting for Bob to come out. He locked himself up again and never went out all night. God knows when she went home. The next day she turned up again and screamed at me to make him go back to her and their daughter. Fine set-out that was. I'll never forget it.'

'As a result,' said Wexford, 'you gave him the sack.'

'I never did! Is that what he says?'

Wexford nodded.

'God damn it! Bob Hathall always was a liar. I'll tell you what happened, and you can believe it or not, as you like. I had him in here after all that set-out and told him he'd better manage his private affairs a bit better. We had a bit of an argument and

95

the upshot was he flew into a rage and said he was leaving. I tried to dissuade him. He'd come to us as an office boy and done all his training here. I told him that if he was getting a divorce he'd need all the money he could lay his hands on and there'd be a rise for him in the New Year. But he wouldn't listen, kept saying everyone was against him and this Angela. So he left and got himself some tin-pot part-time job, and serve him right.'

Recalling Angela's fraud and her remark to Paul Craig, and telling himself that birds of a feather flock together, Wexford asked Mr Butler if Robert Hathall had ever done anything which could be construed even mildly as on the shady side of the law. Mr Butler looked shocked.

'Certainly not. I've said he wasn't always strictly truthful, but otherwise he was honest.'

'Susceptible to women, would you say?'

William Butler gave another squawk and shook his head vehemently. 'He was fifteen when he first came here, and even in those days he was walking out with that first wife of his. They were engaged for God knows how many years. I tell you, Bob was so narrow and downright repressed, he didn't know there were other women on the face of the earth. We'd got a pretty typist in here, and for all the notice he took, she might have been a type*writer*. No, that was why he went overboard for that Angela, went daft about her like some silly romantic schoolboy. He woke up, the scales fell from his eyes. It's often the way. Those late developers are always the worst.'

'So perhaps, having awakened, he began looking around some more?'

'Perhaps he did, but I can't help you there. You thinking he might have done away with that Angela?'

'I shouldn't care to commit myself on that, Mr Butler,' said Wexford as he took his leave.

'No. Silly question, eh? I thought he was going to murder that other one, I can tell you. That's just where she had her sit-in, the step you're on now. I'll never forget it, never as long as I live.'

Howard Fortune was a tall thin man, skeletally thin in spite of his enormous appetite. He had the Wexford family's pale hair, the colour of faded brown paper, and the light grey-blue eyes, small and sharp. In spite of the difference in their figures, he had always resembled his uncle, and now that Wexford had lost so much weight, that resemblance was heightened. Sitting opposite each other in Howard's study, they might have been father and son, for, likeness apart, Wexford was now able to talk to his nephew as familiarly as he talked to Burden, and Howard to respond without the delicacy and self-conscious tact of former days.

Their wives were out. Having spent the day shopping, they had adjourned to a theatre, and uncle and nephew had eaten their dinner alone. Now, while Howard drank brandy and he contented himself with a glass of white wine, Wexford enlarged on the theory he had put forward the night before.

'As far as I see it,' he said, 'the only way to account for Hathall's horror – and it was horror, Howard – when I told him about the handprint, is that he arranged the killing of Angela with the help of a woman accomplice.'

'With whom he was having a love affair?'

'Presumably. That would be the motive.'

'A thin motive these days, isn't it? Divorce is fairly easy and there were no children to consider.'

'You've missed the point.' Wexford spoke with a sharpness that would once have been impossible. 'Even with this new job of his, he couldn't have afforded two discarded wives. He's just the sort of man who'd think himself almost justified in killing if killing was going to rid him of further persecution.'

'So this girl-friend of his came to the cottage in the afternoon …'

'Or was fetched by Angela.'

'I can't see that part, Reg.'

'A neighbour, a woman called Lake, says Angela told her she was going out.' Wexford sipped his drink to cover the slight confusion even the mention of Nancy Lake's name caused in him. 'I have to bear that in mind.'

'Well, maybe. The girl killed Angela by strangling her with a gilt necklace which hasn't been found, then wiped the place clean of her own prints but left one on the side of the bath. Is that the idea?'

'That's the idea. Then she drove Robert Hathall's car to London, where she abandoned it in Wood Green. I may go there tomorrow, but I haven't much hope. The chances are she lives as far from Wood Green as possible.'

'And then you'll go to this toy factory place in – what's it called? – Toxborough? I can't understand why you're leaving it till last. He worked there, after all, from the time of his marriage till last July.'

'And that's the very reason why,' said Wexford. 'It's just possible he knew this woman *before* he met Angela, or met her when his marriage was three years old. But there's no doubt he was deeply in love with Angela – everyone admits that – so is it likely he'd have begun a new relationship during the earliest part of his marriage?'

'No, I see that. Does it have to be someone he'd met at work? Why not a friend he'd met socially or the wife of a friend?'

'Because he doesn't seem to have had any friends, and that's not so difficult to understand. In his first marriage, the way I picture it, he and his wife would have been friendly with other married couples. But you know how it goes, Howard. In these cases, a married couple's friends are their neighbours or her woman friends and their husbands. Isn't it probable that at the time of the divorce all these people would have rallied round Eileen Hathall? In other words, they'd remain her friends and desert him.'

'This unknown woman could be someone he'd picked up in the street or got talking to by chance in a pub. Have you thought of that?'

'Of course. If it's so, my chances of finding her are thin.'

'Well, Wood Green for you tomorrow. I'm taking

the day off myself. I have to speak at a dinner at Brighton in the evening and I thought of taking a leisurely drive down, but maybe I'll come up to darkest Ally Pally with you first.'

The phone ringing cut short Wexford's thanks at this offer. Howard picked up the receiver and his first words, spoken cordially but without much familiarity, told his uncle that the caller was someone he knew socially but not very well. Then the phone was passed to him and he heard Burden's voice.

'Good news first,' said the inspector, 'if you can call it good,' and he told Wexford that at last someone had come forward to say he had seen Hathall's car driven into the drive of Bury Cottage at five past three on the previous Friday afternoon. But he had seen only the driver whom he described as a dark-haired young woman wearing some sort of red checked shirt or blouse. That she had a passenger he was sure, and almost sure it had been a woman, but he was able to fill in no more details. He had been cycling along Wool Lane in the direction of Wool Farm and had therefore been on the left-hand side of the road, the side which would naturally give him a view of the car's driver but not necessarily of the other occupant. The car had stopped since he had the right of way, and he had assumed, because its right-hand indicator was flashing, that it was about to turn into the cottage drive.

'Why didn't this cyclist guy come forward before?'

'He was on holiday down here, he and his bicycle,'

said Burden, 'and he says he never saw a paper till today.'

'Some people,' Wexford growled, 'live like bloody chrysalises. If that's the good news, what's the bad?'

'It may not be bad, I wouldn't know. But the chief constable's been in here after you, and he wants to see you at three sharp tomorrow afternoon.'

'That puts paid to our Wood Green visit,' said Wexford thoughtfully to his nephew, and he told him what Burden had said. 'I'll have to go back and try and take in Croydon or Toxborough on my way. I shan't have time for both.'

'Look, Reg, why don't I drive you to Croydon and then to Kingsmarkham via Toxborough? I'd still have three or four hours before I need to be in Brighton.'

'Be a bit of a drag for you, won't it?'

'On the contrary. I don't mind telling you I'm very keen to take a look at this virago, the first Mrs Hathall. You come back with me and Dora can stay on. I know Denise wants her to be here on Friday for some party or other she's going to.'

And Dora, who came in ten minutes later, needed no encouragement to remain in London till the Sunday.

'But will you be all right on your own?'

'I'll be all right. I hope you will. Personally, I should think you'll perish with the cold in this bloody awful air-conditioning.'

'I have my subcutaneous fat, darling, to keep me warm.'

'Unlike you, Uncle Reg,' said Denise who, coming in, had heard the last sentence. 'All yours has melted away quite beautifully. I suppose it really *is* all diet? I was reading in a book the other day that men who have a succession of love affairs keep their figures because a man unconsciously draws in his stomach muscles every time he pays court to a new woman.'

'So now we know what to think,' said Dora.

But Wexford, who had at that moment drawn his in consciously, wasn't brought to the blush which would have been his reaction the day before. He was wondering what he was to think of his summons by the chief constable, and making a disagreeable guess at the answer.

10

The house which Robert Hathall had bought at the time of his marriage was one of those semi-detached villas which sprang up during the thirties in their thousands, in their tens of thousands. It had a bay window in the front living room, a gable over the front bedroom window, and a decorative wooden canopy, of the kind sometimes seen sheltering the platforms of provincial railway stations, over the front door. There were about four hundred others exactly like it in the street, a wide thoroughfare along which traffic streamed to the south.

'This house,' said Howard, 'was built for about six hundred pounds. Hathall would have paid around four thousand for it, I should think. When did he get married?'

'Seventeen years ago.'

'Four thousand would be right. And now it would fetch eighteen.'

'Only he can't sell it,' said Wexford. 'I daresay he could have done with eighteen thousand pounds.' They got out of the car and went up to the front door.

She had none of the outward signs of a virago. She was about forty, short, high-coloured, her stout stocky figure crammed into a tight green dress, and she was one of those women who have been roses and are now cabbages. Ghostly shades of the rose showed in the pretty fat-obscured features, the skin which was still good, and the gingery hair that had once been blonde. She took them into the room with the bay window. Its furnishings lacked the charm of those at Bury Cottage, but it was just as clean. There was something oppressive about its neatness and the absence of any single object not totally conventional. Wexford looked in vain for some article, a hand-embroidered cushion maybe, an original drawing or a growing plant, that might express the personalities of the woman and the girl who lived here. But there was nothing, not a book, not a magazine even, no paraphernalia of a hobby. It was like a Times Furnishing window display before the shop assistant has added those touches that will give it an air of home. Apart from a framed photograph, the only picture was that reproduction of a Spanish gypsy with a black hat on her curls and a rose between her teeth, which Wexford had seen on a hundred lounge-bar walls. And even this stereotyped picture had more life about it than the rest of the room, the gypsy's mouth seeming to curl a little more disdainfully as she surveyed the sterile surroundings in which she was doomed to spend her time.

Although it was mid-morning and Eileen Hathall had been forewarned of their coming, she offered them nothing to drink. Her mother-in-law's ways had either rubbed off on her or else her own lack of hospitality had been one of the traits which so endeared the old woman to her. But that Mrs Hathall senior had been deluded in other respects soon showed. Far from keeping 'herself to herself', Eileen was ready to be bitterly expansive about her private life.

At first, however, she was subdued. Wexford began by asking her how she had spent the previous Friday, and she replied in a quiet reasonable voice that she had been at her father's in Balham, remaining there till the evening because her daughter had been on a day trip to France, sponsored by her school, from which she hadn't returned until nearly midnight. She gave Wexford her widowed father's address which Howard, who knew London well, remarked was in the next street to where Mrs Hathall senior lived. That did it. Eileen's colour rose and her eyes smouldered with the resentment which was now perhaps the mainspring of her life.

'We grew up together, Bob and me. We went to the same school and there wasn't a day went by we didn't see each other. After we got married we were never apart for a single night till that woman came and stole him from me.'

Wexford, who held to the belief that it is impossible for an outsider to break up a secure and happy marriage, made no comment. He had often wondered too at the attitude of mind that regards people as things and marriage partners as objects which can be stolen like television sets or pearl necklaces.

'When did you last see your former husband, Mrs Hathall?'

'I haven't seen him for three and a half years.'

'But I suppose, although you have custody, he has reasonable access to Rosemary?'

Her face had grown bitter, a canker eating the blown rose. 'He was allowed to see her every other Sunday. I used to send her round to his mum and he'd fetch her from there and take her out for the day.'

'But you didn't see him yourself on these occasions?'

She looked down, perhaps to hide her humiliation. 'He said he wouldn't come if I was going to be there.'

'You said "used", Mrs Hathall. D'you mean this meeting between father and daughter has ceased?'

'Well, she's nearly grown-up, isn't she? She's old enough to have a mind of her own. Me and Bob's mum, we've always got on well, she's been like another mother to me. Rosemary could see the way we thought about it – I mean, she was old enough to understand what I'd suffered from her dad, and it's only natural she was resentful.' The virago was appearing and the tone of voice which Mr Butler had said would always remain in his memory. 'She took against him. She thought it was wicked what he'd done.'

'So she stopped seeing him?'

'She didn't *want* to see him. She said she'd got better things to do with her Sundays, we thought she was quite right. Only once she went to that cottage place and when she came back she was in an awful state, tears and sobbing and I don't know what. And I don't wonder. Can you imagine a father actually letting his little girl see him kiss another woman? That's what happened. When the time came for him to bring Rosemary back, she saw him put his arms round that woman and kiss her. And it wasn't one of your ordinary kisses. Like what you'd see on the TV, Rosemary said, but I won't go into details, though I was disgusted, I can tell you. The upshot of it was that Rosemary can't stand her dad, and I don't blame her. I just hope it won't do something to her mentality the way these psychological people say it does.'

The red flush on her skin was high now and her eyes flashed. And now, as her bosom rose and she tossed her head, she had something in common with the gypsy on the wall.

'*He* didn't like it. He begged her to see him, wrote her letters and God knows what. Sent her presents and wanted to take her away on holiday. Him as said he hadn't got a penny to bless himself with. Fought tooth and nail he did to try and stop me getting this house and a bit of his money to live on. Oh, he's got money enough when he likes to spend it, money to spend on anyone but me.'

Howard had been looking at that single framed photograph and now he asked if it was of Rosemary.

'Yes, that's my Rosemary.' Still breathless from her outpouring of invective, Eileen spoke in gasps. 'That was taken six months ago.'

The two policemen looked at the portrait of a rather plain heavy-faced girl who wore a small gold cross hanging against her blouse, whose lank dark hair fell to her shoulders, and who bore a marked resemblance to her paternal grandmother. Wexford, who felt unable to tell an outright lie and say the girl was pretty, asked what she was going to do when she left school. This was a good move, for it had a calming effect on Eileen whose bitterness gave way, though only briefly, to pride.

'Go on to college. All her teachers say she's got it in her and I wouldn't stand in her way. It's not as if she's got to go out and earn money. Bob'll have plenty to spare *now*. I've told her I don't care if she goes on training till she's twenty-five. I'm going to get Bob's mum to ask him to give Rosemary a car for her eighteenth birthday. After all, that's like being twenty-one nowadays, isn't it? My brother's been teaching her to drive and she'll take her test the minute she's seventeen. It's his duty to give her a car. Just because he's ruined my life, that's no reason why he should ruin hers, is it?'

Wexford put out his hand to her as they left. She gave him hers rather reluctantly, but her reluctance was perhaps only part and parcel of that ungraciousness which seemed to be a feature of all the Hathalls and all their connections. Staring down, he held it just long enough to make sure there was no scar on the relevant finger.

'Let us be thankful for our wives,' said Howard devoutly when they were back in the car and driving southwards. 'He didn't kill Angela to go back to that one, at any rate.'

'Did you notice she didn't once mention Angela's death? Not even to say she wasn't sorry she was dead? I've never come across a family so nourished on hatred.' Wexford thought suddenly of his own two daughters who loved him, and on whose education he had spent money freely and happily because they loved him and he loved them. 'It must be bloody awful to have to support someone you hate and buy presents for someone who's been taught to hate you,' he said.

'Indeed it must. And where did the money come from for those presents and that projected holiday, Reg? Not out of fifteen pounds a week.'

By a quarter to twelve they were in Toxborough. Wexford's appointment at Kidd's factory was for half past, so they had a quick lunch in a pub on the outskirts before finding the industrial site. The factory, a large white concrete box, was the source of those children's toys which he had often seen on television commercials and which were marketed under the name of Kidd's Kits for Kids. The manager, a Mr Aveney, told him they had three hundred workers on the payroll, most of them women with part-time jobs. Their white-collar staff was small, consisting of himself, the personnel manager, the part-time accountant, Hathall's successor, his own secretary, two typists and a switchboard girl.

'You want to know what female office staff we had here when Mr Hathall was with us. I gathered that from what you said on the phone and I've done my best to make you a list of names and addresses. But the way they change and change about is ridiculous, Chief Inspector. Girls are crazy to change their jobs every few months these days. There isn't anyone in the office now who was here when Mr Hathall was here, and he's only been gone ten weeks. Not girls, that is. The personnel manager's been with us for five years, but his office is down in the works and I don't think they ever met.'

'Can you remember if he was particularly friendly with any girl?'

'I can remember he wasn't,' said Mr Aveney. 'He was crazy about that wife of his, the one who got herself killed. I never heard a man go on about a woman the way he went on about her. She was Marilyn Monroe and the Shah-ess of Persia and the Virgin Mary all rolled in one as far as he was concerned.'

But Wexford was tired of hearing about Robert Hathall's uxoriousness. He glanced at the list, formidably long, and there were the names, the sort of names they all seemed to have these days, Junes and Janes and Susans and Lindas and Julies. They had all lived in and around Toxborough and not one of them had stayed at Kidd's more than six months. He had a horrible prevision of weeks of work while half a dozen men scoured the Home Counties for this Jane, this Julie, this Susan, and then he put the list in his briefcase.

'Your friend said he'd like to have a look round the works, so if you'd care to, we'll go down and find him.'

They found Howard in the custody of a Julie who was leading him between benches where women in overalls and with turbans round their heads were peeling the casts from plastic dolls. The factory was airy and pleasant, apart from the smell of cellulose, and from a couple of speakers came the seductive voice of Engelbert Humperdinck imploring his listeners to release him and let him love again.

'A bit of a dead loss that,' said Wexford when they had said good-bye to Mr Aveney. 'I thought it would be. Still, you'll be in plenty of time for your dinner date. It's no more than half an hour from here to Kingsmarkham. And I shall be in time to get myself promptly hauled over the coals. Would you like me to direct you round the back doubles so that we can miss the traffic and I can show you one or two points of interest?'

Howard said he would, so his uncle instructed him how to find the Myringham Road. They went through the centre of the town and past that shopping precinct whose ugliness had so offended Mark Somerset and where he had met the Hathalls on their shopping spree.

'Follow the signs for Pomfret rather than Kingsmarkham, and then I'll direct you into Kingsmarkham via Wool Lane.'

Obediently, Howard followed the signs and within

ten minutes they were in country lanes. Here was unspoilt country, the soft Sussex of undulating hills topped with tree rings, of acres of fir forest and little brown-roofed farms nestling in woody hollows. The harvest was in, and where the wheat had been cut the fields were a pale blond, shining like sheets of silver gilt in the sun.

'When I'm out here,' said Howard, 'I feel the truth of what Orwell said about every man knowing in his heart that the loveliest thing to do in the world is to spend a fine day in the country. And when I'm in London I agree with Charles Lamb.'

'D'you mean preferring to see a theatre queue than all the flocks of silly sheep on Epsom Downs?'

Howard laughed and nodded. 'I take it I'm to avoid that turn that says Sewingbury?'

'You want the right turn for Kingsmarkham, coming up in about a mile. It's a little side road and eventually it becomes Wool Lane. I think Angela must have come along here in the car with her passenger last Friday. But where did she come *from*?'

Howard took the turn. They passed Wool Farm and saw the sign Wool Lane, at which the road became a narrow tunnel. If they had met another car, its driver or Howard would have had to pull right up on to the bank to allow the other's passage, but they met no cars. Motorists avoided the narrow perilous lane and few strangers took it for a through road at all.

'Bury Cottage,' Wexford said.

Howard slowed slightly. As he did so, Robert

112

Hathall came round from the side of the house with a pair of garden shears in his hands. He didn't look up, but began chopping the heads off Michaelmas daisies. Wexford wondered if his mother had nagged him into this unaccustomed task.

'That's him,' he said. 'Did you get a look?'

'Enough to identify him again,' said Howard, 'though I don't suppose I shall have to.'

They parted at the police station. The chief constable's Rover was already parked on the forecourt. He was early for his appointment but so was Wexford. There was no need to rush up breathless and penitent, so he took his time about it, walking in almost casually to where the carpet and the coals awaited him.

'I can guess what it's about, sir. Hathall's been complaining.'

'That you can guess,' said Charles Griswold, 'only makes it worse.' He frowned and drew himself up to his full height which was a good deal more than Wexford's own six feet. The chief constable bore an uncanny likeness to the late General de Gaulle, whose initials he shared, and he must have been aware of it. A chance of nature may account for a physical resemblance to a famous man. Only knowledge of that resemblance, the continual reminders of it from friends and enemies, can account for similarities of the one personality to the other. Griswold was in the habit of speaking of Mid-Sussex, his area, in much the same tones as the dead statesman had spoken of *La France*. 'He's sent me a very strongly worded letter of complaint. Says you've been trying to trap him, using unorthodox methods. Sprang something about a fingerprint on him and then walked out of the house without waiting for his answer. Have you got any grounds for thinking he killed his wife?'

'Not with his own hands, sir. He was in his London office at the time?'

'Then what the hell are you playing at? I am proud of Mid-Sussex. My life's work has been devoted to Mid-Sussex. I was proud of the rectitude of my officers in Mid-Sussex, confident that their conduct might not only be beyond reproach but seen to be beyond reproach.' Griswold sighed heavily. In a moment, Wexford thought, he would be saying, '*L'état, c'est moi.*' 'Why are you harassing this man? Persecuting is what he calls it.'

'Persecuting,' said Wexford, 'is what he always calls it.'

'And that means?'

'He's paranoid, sir.'

'Don't give me that headshrinkers' jargon, Reg. Have you got one single piece of concrete evidence against this chap?'

'No. Only my personal and very strong feeling that he killed his wife.'

'Feeling? Feeling? We hear a damn sight too much about feelings these days and at your age you ought to bloody know better. What d'you mean then, that he had an accomplice? Have you got a *feeling* who this accomplice might be? Have you got any evidence about *him*?'

What could he say but 'No, sir, I haven't? He added more firmly, 'May I see his letter?'

'No, you mayn't,' Griswold snapped. 'I've told you what's in it. Be thankful I'm sparing you his uncomplimentary remarks about your manners and your tactics. He says you've stolen a book of his.'

'For Christ's sake ... You don't believe that?'

'Well, no, Reg, I don't. But have it sent back to him and fast. And lay off him pronto, d'you get that?'

'Lay off him?' said Wexford aghast. 'I have to talk to him. There's no other line of investigation I can pursue.'

'I said lay off him. That's an order. I won't have any more of it. I will not have the reputation of Mid-Sussex sacrificed to your *feelings*.'

11

It was this which marked the end of Wexford's official investigation into the death of Angela Hathall.

Later, when he looked back, he was aware that three twenty-one on the afternoon of Thursday, 2 October, was the moment when all hope of solving her murder in a straightforward above-board way died. But at the time he didn't know that. He felt only grievance and anger, and he resigned himself to the delays and irritations which must ensue if Hathall couldn't be directly pursued. He still thought ways were open to him of discovering the identity of the woman without arousing fresh annoyance in Hathall. He could delegate. Burden and Martin could make approaches of a more tactful nature. Men could be put on the trail of those girls on Aveney's list. In a roundabout way it could be done. Hathall had betrayed himself, Hathall was guilty – therefore, the crime could ultimately be brought home to Hathall.

But he was disheartened. On his way back to Kingsmarkham he had considered phoning Nancy Lake, taking advantage – to put it into plain words – of Dora's absence, but even an innocent dinner with her, envisaged now, lost the savour the prospect of it had had. He didn't get in touch with her. He didn't phone Howard. He spent the lonely weekend of a grass widower, fulminating to himself about Hathall's good luck and about his own folly in being careless in his handling of an irritable and prickly personality.

Of Men and Angels was sent back, accompanied by a printed card on which Wexford had written a polite note regretting having kept it so long. No response came from Hathall, who must, the chief inspector thought, have been rubbing his hands with glee.

On Monday morning he went back to Kidd's factory at Toxborough.

Mr Aveney seemed pleased to see him – those who cannot be incriminated usually take a virtuous pleasure in their involvement in police enquiries – but he couldn't offer much help. 'Other women Mr Hathall might have met here?' he asked.

'I was thinking about sales reps. After all, it's children's toys you make.'

'The sales reps all work from our London office.

117

There's only one woman among them and he never met her. What about those girls' names I gave you? No luck?'

Wexford shook his head. 'Not so far.'

'You won't. There's nothing there. That only leaves the cleaners. We've got one cleaning woman who's been here since we started up, but she's sixty-two. Of course she has a couple of girls working with her, but they're always changing like the rest of our staff. I suppose I *could* give you another list of names. I never see them and Mr Hathall wouldn't have. They've finished before we come in. The only one I can recall offhand I remember because she was so honest. She stayed behind one morning to hand me a pound note she'd found under someone's desk.'

'Don't bother with the list, Mr Aveney,' said Wexford. 'There's obviously nothing there.'

'You've got Hathall-itis,' said Burden as the second week after Angela's death came to an end.

'Sounds like bad breath.'

'I've never known you so – well, I was going to say pigheaded. You haven't got a scrap of evidence that Hathall so much as took another woman out, let alone conspired with her to do murder.'

'That handprint,' said Wexford obstinately, 'and those long dark hairs and that woman seen with Angela in the car.'

'He *thought* it was a woman. How many times have you and I seen someone across the street and not been able to make up our minds whether it was a boy or a girl? You always say the Adam's apple is the one sure distinguishing mark. Does a cyclist glancing into a car notice if the passenger's got an Adam's apple? We've followed up all the girls on that list, bar the one that's in the United States and the one who was in hospital on the nineteenth. Most of them could hardly remember who Hathall is.'

'What's your idea then? How do you account for that print on the bath?'

'I'll tell you. It was a bloke killed Angela. She was lonely and she picked him up like you said at first. He strangled her – by accident maybe – while he was trying to get the necklace off her. Why should he leave prints? Why should he touch anything in the house – except Angela? If he did, there wouldn't have been many and he could have wiped them off. The woman who left the print, she's not even involved. She was a passer-by, a motorist, who called and asked to use the phone ...'

'And the loo?'

'Why not? These things happen. A similar thing happened in my own home yesterday. My daughter was in on her own and a young fellow who'd walked from Stowerton because he couldn't hitch a lift, came and asked for a drink of water. She let him in – I had something to say about that, as you can imagine – and she let him use the bathroom too. Luckily, he was OK and no harm was done. But why shouldn't something like that have happened at Bury Cottage? The woman hasn't come forward because she doesn't even know the name of the house she called at or the name of the woman who let her in. Her prints aren't on the phone or anywhere else because Angela was still cleaning the place when she called. Isn't that more reasonable than this conspiracy idea that hasn't the slightest foundation?'

Griswold liked the theory. And Wexford found himself in charge of an enquiry based on a postulation he couldn't for a moment believe in. He was obliged to give his support to a nation-wide hue and cry aimed at locating an amnesiac female motorist and a thief who killed by chance for a valueless necklace. Neither were found, neither took more definite shape than the vague outlines Burden had invented for them, but Griswold and Burden and the newspapers talked about them as if they existed. And Robert Hathall, Wexford learned at second-hand, had made a series of helpful suggestions as to one fresh lead after another. The chief constable couldn't understand – so the grass roots had it – what had given rise to the idea that the man suffered from a persecution complex or was bad-tempered. Nothing could have been more cooperative than his attitude once Wexford was removed from direct contact with him.

Wexford thought he would soon grow sick of the whole thing. The weeks dragged on and there were no new developments. At first it is maddening to have one's certain knowledge discounted and derided. Then, as fresh interests and fresh work enter, it becomes merely annoying; lastly, a bore. Wexford would have been very happy to have regarded Robert Hathall as a bore. After all, no one solves every murder case. Dozens have always, and always will have, eluded solution. Right should, of course, be done and justice hold sway, but the human element makes this impossible. Some must get away and Hathall was evidently going to be one of them. He ought by now to have been relegated to the ranks of the bores, for he wasn't an interesting man but essentially an irritating humourless bore. Yet Wexford couldn't think of him as such. In himself, he might be tedious but what he had done was not. Wexford wanted to know why he had done it and how and with what help and by what means. And above all he felt a righteous indignation that a man might kill his wife and bring his mother to find her body and yet be regarded by the powers-that-be as *co-operative*.

He mustn't let this thing develop into an obsession. He reminded himself that he was a reasonable, level-headed man, a policeman with a job to do, not an executioner impelled to the hunt by some political mission or holy cause. Perhaps it was those months of starving himself that had robbed him of his steadiness, his equanimity. But only a fool would gain a good figure at the price of an unbalanced mind. Reminding himself of this excellent maxim, he kept cool when Burden told him Hathall was about to give up his tenancy of Bury Cottage, and replied with sarcasm rather than explosively.

'I suppose I'm to be allowed to know where he's going?'

Burden had been considered by Griswold as having a nice line in tact and had therefore, throughout the autumn, been the link with Hathall. The Mid-Sussex envoy was what Wexford called him, adding that he imagined 'our man' in Wool

Lane would be in possession of such top-level secrets.

'He's staying with his mother in Balham for the time being and he talks of getting a flat in Hampstead.'

'The vendor will cheat him,' said Wexford bitterly, 'the train service will be appalling. He'll be made to pay an extortionate rent for his garage and someone's going to put up a tower block that'll spoil his view of the Heath. All in all, he'll be very happy.'

'I don't know why you make him out such a masochist.'

'I make him out a murderer.'

'Hathall didn't murder his wife,' said Burden. 'He's just got an unfortunate manner that got in your hair.'

'An unfortunate manner! Why not be blunt about it and say he has fits? He's allergic to fingerprints. Mention you've found one on his bath and he has an epileptic seizure.'

'You'd hardly call that evidence, would you?' said Burden rather coldly, and he put on his glasses for no better reason, Wexford thought, than to peer censoriously through them at his superior officer.

But the idea of Hathall's departing and beginning the new life he had planned for himself and done murder to achieve was a disturbing one. That it had been allowed to happen was almost entirely due to his own mishandling of the investigation. He had spoilt things by being tough with and rude to the kind of man who would never respond to such treatment. And now there was nothing more he could do because Hathall's person was sacrosanct and every clue to the unknown woman's identity locked up in his sacrosanct mind. Was there any point in learning Hathall's new address? If he wasn't permitted to talk to him in Kingsmarkham, what hope had he of breaching his London privacy? For a long time personal pride stopped him asking Burden for news of Hathall, and Burden offered none until one day in spring, when they were lunching together at the Carousel. The inspector dropped Hathall's new address casually into their conversation, prefacing his remark with a 'by the by', as if he were speaking of some slight acquaintance of theirs, a man in whom neither could have more than a passing interest.

'So now he tells me,' said Wexford to the tomato-shaped sauce bottle.

'There doesn't seem to be any reason why you shouldn't know.'

'Got it okayed by the Home Secretary first, did you?'

Having the address didn't really help matters and its location meant very little to Wexford. He was prepared to drop the subject there and then, knowing as he did that discussing Hathall with Burden only made them both feel awkward. Strangely enough, it was Burden who pursued it. Perhaps he hadn't cared for that crack about the Home Secretary or, more likely, disliked the idea of the significance that might attach to his announcement if he left it islanded.

'I've always thought,' he said, 'though I haven't said so before, that there was one major drawback to your theory. If Hathall had an accomplice with that scar on her finger, he'd have insisted she wear gloves. Because if she left only one print, he'd never be able to live with her or marry her or even see her again. And you say he killed Angela in order to do that. So he can't have. It's simple when you think about it.'

Wexford didn't say anything. He betrayed no excitement. But that night when he got home he studied his map of London, made a phone call and spent some time poring over his latest bank statement.

The Fortunes had come to stay for the weekend. Uncle and nephew walked down Wool Lane and paused outside the cottage which hadn't yet been re-let. The 'miracle' tree was laden with white blossom, and behind the house young lambs were pastured on the hillside whose peak was crowned by a ring of trees.

'Hathall doesn't prefer the flocks of silly sheep either,' said Wexford, recalling a conversation they had had near this spot. 'He's taken himself as far from Epsom Downs as can be, yet he's a South Londoner. West Hampstead is where he's living. Dartmeet Avenue. D'you know it?'

'I know where it is. Between the Finchley Road and West End Lane. Why did he pick Hampstead?'

'Just because it's as far as possible from South London where his mother and his ex-wife and his daughter are.' Wexford pulled down a branch of plum blossom to his face and smelt its faint honey scent. 'Or that's what *I think*.' The branch sprang back, scattering petals on the grass. Musingly, he said, 'He appears to lead a celibate life. The only woman he's been seen with is his mother.'

Howard seemed intrigued. 'You mean you have a – a watcher?'

'He's not much of a spy,' Wexford admitted, 'but he was the best and safest I could find. As a matter of fact, he's the brother of an old customer of mine, a chap called Monkey Matthews. The brother's name is Ginge, so-called on account of his hair. He lives in Kilburn.'

Howard laughed, but sympathetically. 'What does this Ginge do? Tail him?'

'Not exactly. But he keeps an eye. I give him a remuneration. Out of my own pocket, naturally.'

'I didn't realize you were that serious.'

'I don't know when I was ever so serious about a thing like this in my whole career.'

They turned away. A little wind had sprung up and it was growing chilly. Howard gave a backward glance at the hedge tunnel which was already greening and thickening, and said quietly, 'What is it you hope for, Reg?'

His uncle didn't reply at once. They had passed the isolated villa where Nancy Lake's car stood on the garage drive, before he spoke. He had been deep in thought, so silent and preoccupied that Howard had perhaps thought he had forgotten the question or had no answer to it. But now as they came to the Stowerton Road, he said, 'For a long time I wondered why Hathall was so horrified – and that's an understatement – when I told him about the print. Because he didn't want the woman discovered, of course. But it wasn't just fear he showed. It was something more like a terrible sorrow he showed – when he'd recovered a bit, that is. And I came to the conclusion that his reaction was what it was because he'd had Angela killed expressly so that he could be with that woman. And now he knew he'd never dare see her again.

'And then he reflected. He wrote that letter of protest to Griswold to clear the field of me because he knew I knew. But it might still be possible for him to get away with it and have what he wanted, a life with that woman. Not as he'd planned it. Not a flit to London, then after a few weeks a friendship with a girl, the lonely widower seeking consolation with a new woman friend whom, as time went by, he could marry. Not that – now. Even though he'd pulled the wool over Griswold's eyes, he wouldn't dare try that one on. The handprint had been found and however much we might seem to be ignoring him, he couldn't hope to go in for a public courtship and then marriage with a woman whose hand would betray her. Betray her to anyone, Howard, not just to an expert.'

'So what can he do?'

'He has two alternatives,' said Wexford crisply. 'He and the woman may have agreed to part. Presumably, even if one is madly in love, liberty is preferable to the indulgence of love. Yes, they could have parted.'

'"Shake hands for ever, cancel all our vows"?'

'The next bit is even more appropriate.
"And if we meet at any time again,
Be it not seen in either of our brows
That we one jot of former love retain."'

'Or,' Wexford went on, 'they could have decided – let's say grandiloquently that their passion decided for them, love was bigger than both of them – to have gone on meeting clandestinely. Not to live together, never to meet in public, but to carry on as if each of them had a jealous suspicious spouse.'

'What, go on like that indefinitely?'

'Maybe. Until it wears itself out or until they find some other solution. But I think that's what they're doing, Howard. If it isn't so, why has he picked North-west London where no one knows him as a place to live? Why not south of the river where his mother is and his daughter? Or somewhere near his work. He's earning a good salary now. He could just as well have got himself a place in Central London. He's hidden himself away so that he can sneak out in the evenings to be with *her*.

'I'm going to try and find her,' Wexford said thoughtfully. 'It'll cost me some money and take up my spare time, but I mean to have a go.'

12

In describing Ginge Matthews as not much of a spy, Wexford had rather underrated him. The miserable resources at his disposal made him bitter. He was perpetually irritated by Ginge's unwillingness to use the phone. Ginge was proud of his literary style which was culled from the witness-box manner of thick-headed and very junior police constables whose periphrasis he had overheard from the dock. In Ginge's reports his quarry never went anywhere, but always proceeded; his home was his domicile and, rather than going home, he withdrew or retired there. But in honesty and in fairness to Ginge, Wexford had to admit that, although he had learnt nothing of the elusive woman during these past months, he had learnt a good deal about Hathall's manner of life.

According to Ginge, the house where he had his flat was a big three-storeyed place and – reading between the lines – of Edwardian vintage. Hathall had no garage but left his car parked in the street. From meanness or the impossibility of finding a garage to rent? Wexford didn't know and Ginge couldn't tell him. Hathall left for work at nine in the morning and either walked or caught a bus from West End Green to West Hampstead Tube station where he took the Bakerloo Line train to (presumably) Piccadilly. He reached home again soon after six, and on several occasions Ginge, lurking in a phone box opposite number 62 Dartmeet Avenue, had seen him go out again in his car. Ginge always knew when he was at home in the evenings because then a light showed in the second floor bay window. He had never seen him accompanied by anyone except his mother – from his description it could only be old Mrs Hathall – whom he had brought to his flat by car one Saturday afternoon. Mother and son had had words, a harsh low-voiced quarrel on the pavement before they even got to the front door.

Ginge had no car. He had no job either, but the small amount of money Wexford could afford to give him didn't make it worth his while to spend more than one evening and perhaps one Saturday or Sunday afternoon a week watching Robert Hathall. It could easily have happened that Hathall brought his girl home on one or two of the other six evenings. And yet Wexford clung to hope. One day, sometime … He dreamed at night of Hathall, not very often, possibly once a fortnight, and in these dreams he saw him with the dark-haired girl with the scarred finger, or else alone as he had been when he had stood by the fireplace in Bury Cottage, paralysed with fear and realization and – yes, with grief.

'On the afternoon of Saturday, June 15th inst., at 3.5 p.m., the party was seen to proceed from his domicile at 62 Dartmeet Avenue to West End Lane where he made purchases at a supermarket ...' Wexford cursed. They were nearly all like that. And what proof had he that Ginge had even been there 'on the afternoon of Saturday, June 15th inst.'? Naturally, Ginge would say he had been there when there was a quid in it for every tailing session. July came and August, and Hathall, if Ginge was to be trusted, led a simple regular life, going to work, coming home, shopping on Saturdays, sometimes taking an evening drive. If Ginge could be trusted ...

That he could be, up to a point, was proved in September just before the anniversary of Angela's death. 'There is reason to believe', wrote Ginge, 'that the party has disposed of his motor vehicle, it having disappeared from its customary parking places. On the evening of Thursday, September 10th inst., having arrived home from his place of business at 6.10 p.m., he proceeded at 6.50 from his domicile and boarded the number 28 bus at West End Green NW6.'

Was there anything in it? Wexford didn't think so. On his salary Hathall could easily afford to run a car, but he might have got rid of it only because of the increasing difficulty of on-street parking. Still, it was a good thing from his point of view. Hathall could now be followed.

Wexford never wrote to Ginge. It was too risky. The little red-headed spy might not be above blackmail, and if any letters should fall into the hands of Griswold ... He sent his wages in notes in a plain envelope, and when he had to talk to him, which, on account of the paucity of news, happened rarely, he could always get him between twelve and one at a Kilburn public house called the Countess of Castlemaine.

'Follow him?' said Ginge nervously. 'What, on that bleeding 28?'

'I don't see why not. He's never seen you, has he?'

'Maybe he has. How should I know? It's not easy following a bloke on a bleeding bus.' Ginge's conversational manner was markedly different from his literary style, particularly as to his use of adjectives. 'If he goes up top, say, and I go inside, or vicey-versy ...'

'Why does there have to be any vicey-versy?' said Wexford. 'You sit in the seat behind him and stick close. Right?'

Ginge didn't seem to think it was right at all, but he agreed rather dubiously to try it. Whether or not he had tried it, Wexford wasn't told, for Ginge's next report made no reference to buses. Yet the more he studied it with its magistrates' court circumlocutions, the more interested he was by it. 'Being in the neighbourhood of Dartmeet Avenue

NW6, at 3 p.m. on the 26th inst., I took it upon myself to investigate the party's place of domicile. During a conversation with the landlord, during which I represented myself as an official of the local rating authority, I enquired as to the number of apartments and was informed that only single rooms were to let in the establishment ...'

Rather enterprising of Ginge, was Wexford's first thought, though he had probably only assumed this role to impress his employer and hope he would forget about the more dangerous exercise of tailing Hathall on a bus. But that wasn't important. What astonished the chief inspector was that Hathall was a tenant rather than an owner-occupier and, moreover, the tenant of a room rather than a flat. Strange, very strange. He could have afforded to buy a flat on a mortgage. Why hadn't he? Because he didn't intend to be permanently domiciled (as Ginge would put it) in London? Or because he had other uses for his income? Both maybe. But Wexford seized upon this as the most peculiar circumstance he had yet discovered in Hathall's present life. Even with rents in London as extortionate as they were, he could hardly be paying more than fifteen pounds a week at the most for a room, yet, after deductions, he must be drawing sixty. Wexford had no confidant but Howard, and it was to Howard, on the phone, that he talked about it.

'You're thinking he could be supporting someone else?'

'I am,' said Wexford.

'Say fifteen a week for himself and fifteen for her

on accommodation ...? And if she's not working he has to keep her as well.'

'Christ, you don't know how good it is for me to hear someone talk about her as a real person, as "she". You believe she exists, don't you?'

'It wasn't a ghost made that print, Reg. It wasn't ectoplasm. She exists.'

In Kingsmarkham they had given up. They had stopped searching. Griswold had told the newspapers some rubbish – in Wexford's phrase – about the case not being closed, but it *was* closed. His statement was only face-saving. Mark Somerset had let Bury Cottage to a couple of young Americans, teachers of political economy at the University of the South. The front garden was tidied up and they talked of having the back garden landscaped at their own expense. One day the plums hung heavily on the tree, the next it was stripped. Wexford never found out if Nancy Lake had had them and made them into 'miracle' jam, for he had never seen Nancy since the day he was told to lay off Hathall.

Nothing came from Ginge for a fortnight. At last Wexford phoned him at the Countess of Castlemaine to be told that on his watching evenings Hathall had remained at home. He would, however, watch again that night and on the Saturday afternoon. On Monday his report came. Hathall had done his usual shopping on Saturday, but on the previous evening had walked down to the bus stop at West End Green at seven o'clock. Ginge had followed him, but being intimidated ('made cautious' was his expression) by Hathall's suspicious backward glances, hadn't pursued him on to the 28 bus which his quarry had caught at ten past seven. Wexford hurled the sheet of paper into the wastepaper basket. That was all he needed, for Hathall to get wise to Ginge.

Another week went by. Wexford was on the point of throwing Ginge's next communication away unopened. He felt he couldn't face another account of Hathall's Saturday shopping activities. But he did open the letter. And there, of course, was the usual nonsense about the supermarket visit. There too, appended casually as if it were of no importance, a throwaway line to fill up, was a note that after his shopping Hathall had called at a travel agency.

'The place he went to is called Sudamerica Tours, Howard. Ginge didn't dare follow him in, lily-livered idiot that he is.'

Howard's voice sounded thin and dry. 'You're thinking what I'm thinking.'

'Of course. Some place where we've no extradition treaty. He's been reading about train robbers and that gave him the idea. Bloody newspapers do more harm than good.'

'But, my God, Reg, he must be dead scared if he's prepared to throw up his job and flit to Brazil or somewhere. What's he going to do there? How will he live?'

'As birds do, nephew. God knows. Look, Howard, could you do something for me? Could you get on to Marcus Flower and try and find out if they're sending him abroad? I daren't.'

'Well, I dare,' said Howard. 'But if they were,

wouldn't they be arranging the whole thing and paying for it?'

'They wouldn't pay and arrange for his girl, would they?'

'I'll do my best and call you back this evening.'

Was that why Hathall had been living so economically? In order to save up his accomplice's fare? He would have to have a job there waiting for him, Wexford thought, or else be very desperate to get to safety. In that case, the money for two air fares would have to be found. In the *Kingsmarkham Courier*, which had been placed on his desk that morning, he remembered seeing an advertisement for trips to Rio de Janeiro. He fished it out from under a pile of papers and looked at the back page. There it was, the return fare priced at just over three hundred and fifty pounds. Add a bit more for two single fares, and Hathall's saving could be accounted for ...

He was about to discard the newspaper when a name in the deaths column caught his eye. Somerset. 'On October 15th, at Church House, Old Myringham, Gwendolen Mary Somerset, beloved wife of Mark Somerset. Funeral St Luke's Church October 22nd. No flowers, please, but donations to Stowerton Home for Incurables.' So the demanding and querulous wife had died at last. The *beloved* wife? Perhaps she had been, or perhaps this was the usual hypocrisy, so stale, hackneyed and automatic a formula as to be hardly hypocrisy any more. Wexford smiled drily and then forgot about it. He went home early – the town was quiet and crimeless – and waited for Howard's telephone call.

The phone rang at seven, but it was his younger daughter, Sheila. She and her mother chatted for about twenty minutes, and after that the phone didn't ring again. Wexford waited till about half past ten and then he dialled Howard's number.

'He's bloody well out,' he said crossly to his wife. 'I call that the limit.'

'Why shouldn't he go out in the evening? I'm sure he works hard enough.'

'Don't I work? I don't go gallivanting about in the evenings when I've promised to phone people.'

'No, and if you did perhaps your blood pressure wouldn't rage the way it's doing at this moment,' said Dora.

At eleven he tried to get Howard again, but again there was no reply and he went off to bed in a peevish frame of mind. It wasn't surprising that he had another of those obsessive Hathall dreams. He was at an airport. The great jet aircraft was ready to take off and the doors had been closed, but they opened again as he watched and there appeared at the head of the steps, like a royal couple waving graciously to the well-wishing crowd, Hathall and a woman. The woman raised her right hand in a gesture of farewell and he saw the L-shaped scar burning red, an angry cicatrice – L for love, for loss, for leave-taking. But before he could rush up the steps as he had begun to do, the stairs themselves melted away, the couple retreated, and the aircraft sailed up, up into the ice-blue winter sky.

Why is it that as you get older you tend to wake up at five and are unable to get off to sleep again? Something to do with the blood sugar level being low? Or the coming of dawn exerting an atavistic pull? Wexford knew further sleep would elude him, so he got up at half past six and made his own breakfast. He didn't like the idea of phoning Howard before eight, and by a quarter to he was so fidgety and restless that he took a cup of tea in to Dora and went off to work. By now, of course, Howard would have left for Kenbourne Vale. He began to feel bitterly injured, and those old feelings he used to have about Howard reasserted themselves. True, he had listened sympathetically to all his uncle's ramblings about this case, but what was he really thinking? That this was an elderly man's fantasy? Country bumpkin rubbish? It seemed likely that he had only played along to humour him and had deferred that call to Marcus Flower until he could spare the time from his more important metropolitan business. He probably hadn't made it yet. Still, it was no use getting paranoid in Hathall style. He must humble himself, phone Kenbourne Vale and ask again.

This he did at nine-thirty. Howard hadn't yet come in, and he found himself involved in a gossipy chat with Sergeant Clements, an old friend from days when they had worked together on the Kenbourne Vale cemetery murder. Wexford was too kind a man to cut the sergeant short after he had discovered that Howard was delayed at some top-level conference, and resigned himself to hearing all about Clements' adopted son, prospective adopted daughter, and new maisonette. A message would be left for the chief superintendent, Clements said at last, but he wasn't expected in till twelve.

The call finally came at ten past.

'I tried to get you at home before I left,' said Howard, 'but Dora said you'd gone. I haven't had a moment since, Reg.'

There was a note of barely suppressed excitement in his nephew's voice. Maybe he'd been promoted again, Wexford thought, and he said not very warmly, 'You did say you'd phone last night.'

'So I did. At seven. But your line was engaged. I couldn't after that. Denise and I went to the pictures.'

It was the tone of amusement – no, of glee – that did it. Forgetting all about rank, Wexford exploded. 'Charming,' he snapped. 'I hope the people in the row behind you chattered the whole way through and the people in front had it off on the seats and the people in the circle dropped orange peel on you. What about my chap? What about my South America thing?'

'Oh, that,' said Howard, and Wexford could have sworn he heard a yawn. 'He's leaving Marcus Flower, he's resigned. I couldn't get any more.'

'Thanks a lot. And that's all?'

Howard was laughing now. 'Oh, Reg,' he said, 'it's wicked to keep you in suspense, but you were so ripe for it. You're such an irascible old devil, I couldn't resist.' He controlled his laughter and suddenly his voice became solemn, measured. 'That is by no means all,' he said. 'I've seen him.'

'You *what*? D'you mean you've talked to Hathall?'

'No, I've *seen* him. Not alone. With a woman. I've seen him with a woman, Reg.'

'Oh, my God,' said Wexford softly. 'The Lord hath delivered him into mine hands.'

13

'I wouldn't be so sure of that,' said Howard. 'Not yet. But I'll tell you about it, shall I? Funny, isn't it, the way I said I didn't suppose I'd ever have to identify him? But I did identify him last night. Listen, and I'll tell you how it was.'

On the previous evening, Howard had attempted to call his uncle at seven but the line had been engaged. Since he had nothing but negative news for him, he decided to try again in the morning as he was pressed for time. He and Denise were to dine in the West End before going on to the nine o'clock showing of a film at the Curzon Cinema, and Howard had parked his car near the junction of Curzon Street and Half Moon Street. Having a few minutes to spare, he had been drawn by curiosity to have a look at exterior of the offices he had phoned during the day, and he and Denise were approaching the Marcus Flower building when he saw a man and a woman coming towards it from the opposite direction. The man was Robert Hathall.

At the plate-glass window they paused and looked inside, surveying velvet drapery and wall-to-wall Wilton and marble staircase. Hathall seemed to be pointing out to his companion the glossy splendours of the place where he worked. The woman was of medium height, good-looking but not startlingly so, with very short blonde hair. Howard thought she was in her late twenties or early thirties.

'Could the hair have been a wig?' Wexford asked.

'No, but it could have been dyed. Naturally, I didn't see her hand. They were talking to each other in what I thought was an affectionate way and after a bit they walked off down towards Piccadilly. And, incidentally, I didn't enjoy the picture. Under the circumstances, I couldn't concentrate.'

'They haven't shaken hands for ever, Howard. They haven't cancelled all their vows. It's as I thought, and now it can only be a matter of time before we find her.'

The following day was his day of rest, his day off. The ten-thirty train from Kingsmarkham got him to Victoria just before half past eleven and by noon he was in Kilburn. What quirk of romantic imagination had prompted the naming of this squalid Victorian public house after Charles the Second's principal mistress, Wexford couldn't fathom. It stood in a turning off the Edgware Road and it had the air of a gone-to-seed nineteenth-century gin palace. Ginge Matthews was sitting on a stool at the bar in earnest and apparently aggrieved conversation with the Irish barman. When he saw Wexford his eyes widened – or, rather, one eye widened. The other was half-closed and sunk in purple swelling.

'Take your drink over to the corner,' said Wexford. 'I'll join you in a minute. May I have a glass of dry white wine, please?'

Ginge didn't look like his brother or talk like him and he certainly didn't smoke like him, but nevertheless they had something in common apart from their partiality for petty crime. Perhaps one of their parents had been possessed of a dynamic personality, or there might even have been something exceptionally vital in their genes. Whatever it was, it made Wexford say that the Matthews brothers were just like other people only more so. Both were inclined to do things to excess. Monkey smoked sixty king-sized cigarettes a day. Ginge didn't smoke at all but drank, when he could afford it, a concoction of pernod and Guinness.

Ginge hadn't spoken to Monkey for fifteen years and Monkey hadn't spoken to him. They had fallen out as the result of the bungling mess they had made of an attempt to break into a Kingsmarkham furrier's. Ginge had gone to prison and Monkey had not – most unfairly, as Ginge had reasonably thought – and when he came out, the younger brother had taken himself off to London where he had married a widow who owned her own house and a bit of money. Ginge had soon spent the money and she, perhaps in revenge, had presented him with five children. He didn't, therefore, enquire after his brother whom he blamed for many of his misfortunes, but remarked bitterly to Wexford when he joined him at a corner table:

'See my eye?'

'Of course I see it. What the hell have you done to yourself? Walked into your wife's fist?'

'Very funny. I'll tell you who done it. That bleeding Hathall. Last night when I was following him down to the 28 stop.'

'For Christ's sake!' said Wexford, aghast. 'You mean he's on to you?'

'Thanks for the sympathy.' Ginge's small round face flushed nearly as red as his hair. 'Course he was bound to spot me sooner or later on account of my bleeding hair. He hadn't got no cause to turn round and poke me in the bleeding eye, though, had he?'

'Is that what he did?'

'I'm telling you. Cut me, he did. The wife said I looked like Henry Cooper. It wasn't so bleeding funny, I can tell you.'

Wearily, Wexford said, 'Could you stop the bleeding?'

'It stopped in time, naturally, it did. But it isn't healed up yet and you can see the bleeding ...'

'Oh, *God*. I mean stop saying "bleeding" every other word. It's putting me off my drink. Look, Ginge, I'm sorry about your eye, but there's no great harm done. Obviously, you'll have to be a damn sight more careful. For instance, you could try wearing a hat ...'

'I'm not going back there again, Mr Wexford.'

'Never mind that now. Let me buy you another of those what-d'you-call-'ems. What *do* you call them?'

'You ask for a half of draught Guinness with a double pernod in.' Ginge added proudly and more cheerfully, 'I don't know what *they* call 'em but I call 'em Demon Kings.'

The stuff smelt dreadful. Wexford fetched himself another glass of white wine and Ginge said, 'You won't get very fat on that.'

'That's the idea. Now tell me where this 28 bus goes.'

Ginge took a swig of his Demon King and said with extreme rapidity, 'Golders Green, Child's Hill, Fortune Green, West End Lane, West Hampstead Station, Quex Road, Kilburn High Road ...'

'For God's sake! I don't know any of these places, they don't mean a thing to me. Where does it end up?'

'Wandsworth Bridge.'

Disappointed at this disclosure yet pleased for once to be at an advantage in the face of so much sophisticated knowledge, Wexford said, 'He's only going to see his mother in Balham. That's near Balham.'

'Not where that bus goes isn't. Look, Mr Wexford,' said Ginge with patient indulgence, 'you don't know London, you've said so yourself. I've lived here fifteen years and I can tell you nobody as wasn't out of his bleeding twist would go to Balham that way. He'd go to West Hampstead Tube and change on to the Northern at Waterloo or the Elephant. Stands to reason he would.'

'Then he's dropping off somewhere along the route. Ginge, will you do one more thing for me? Is there a pub near this bus stop where you've seen him catch the 28?'

'Oppo-sight,' said Ginge warily.

'We'll give him a week. If he doesn't complain about you during the next week – oh, all right, I know you think you're the one with grounds for complaint – but if he doesn't we'll know he either thinks you're a potential mugger ...'

'Thanks very much.'

'... and doesn't connect you with me,' Wexford went on, ignoring the interruption, 'or else he's too scared at this stage to draw attention to himself. But, beginning next Monday, I want you to station yourself in that pub by six-thirty every night for a week. Just note how often he catches that bus. Will you do that? I don't want you to follow him and you won't be running any risk.'

'That's what you lot always say,' said Ginge. 'You want to remember he's already done some poor bleeder in. Who's going to see after my bleeding wife and kids if he gets throttling me with his bleeding gold chains?'

'The same as look after them now,' said Wexford silkily. 'The Social Security.'

'What a nasty tongue you've got.' For once Ginge sounded exactly like his brother, and briefly he looked like him as a greedy gleam appeared in his good eye. 'What's in it for me if I do?'

'A pound a day,' said Wexford, 'and as many of those – er, bleeding Demon Kings as you can get down you.'

Wexford waited anxiously for another summons from the chief constable, but none came, and by the end of the week he knew that Hathall wasn't going to complain. That, as he had told Ginge, didn't necessarily mean any more than that Hathall thought the man who was following him intended to attack him and had taken the law into his own hands. What was certain, though, was that whatever came out of Ginge's pub observations, he couldn't use the little red-headed man again. And it wasn't going to be much use finding out how often Hathall caught that bus if he could set no one to catch it with him.

Things were very quiet in Kingsmarkham. Nobody would object if he were to take the fortnight's holiday that was owing to him. People who take their summer holidays in November are always popular with colleagues. It all depended on Ginge. If it turned out that Hathall caught that bus regularly, why shouldn't he take his holiday and try to follow that bus by car? It would be difficult in the London traffic, which always intimidated him, but not all that difficult out of the rush hours. And ten to one, a hundred to one, Hathall wouldn't spot him. Nobody on a bus looks at people in cars. Nobody on a bus can *see* the driver of a pursuing car. If only he knew when Hathall was leaving Marcus Flower and when he meant to leave the country ...

But all this was driven out of his head by an event he couldn't have anticipated. He had been certain the weapon would never be found, that it was at the bottom of the Thames or tossed on to some local authority rubbish dump. When the young teacher of political science phoned him to say that a necklace had been found by the men excavating the garden of Bury Cottage and that her landlord, Mr Somerset, had advised her to inform the police, his first thought was that now he could overcome Griswold's scruples, now he could confront Hathall. He had himself driven down Wool Lane – observing on the way the For Sale board outside Nancy Lake's house – and then he walked into the waste land, the area of opencast mining, which had been Hathall's back garden. A load of Westmorland stone made a mountain range in one corner and a mechanical digger stood by the garage. Would Griswold say he should have had this garden dug over? When you're searching for a weapon, you don't dig up a garden that looks just like a bit of field without an exposed, freshly dug bit of earth in the whole of it. There hadn't been even a minuscule break in the long rank grass last September twelvemonth. They had raked over every inch of it. How then had Hathall or his accomplice managed to bury the necklace and restore earth and grass without its being detected?

The teacher, Mrs Snyder, told him.

'There was a kind of cavity under here. A septic

pit, would you call it? I guess Mr Somerset said something about a pit.'

'A cesspit or septic tank,' said Wexford. 'The main drainage came through to this part of Kingsmarkham about twenty years ago, but before that there'd have been a cesspit.'

'For heaven's sake! Why didn't they have it taken out?' said Mrs Snyder with the wonderment of a native of a richer and more hygiene-conscious country. 'Well, this necklace was in it, whatever it's called. That thing …' She pointed to the digger, ' … smashed it open. Or so the workmen said. I didn't look personally. I don't want to seem to criticize your country, Captain, but a thing like that! A cess tank!'

Extremely amused by his new title which made him feel like a naval officer, Wexford said he quite understood that primitive methods of sewage disposal weren't pleasant to contemplate, and where was the necklace?

'I washed it and put it in the kitchen closet. I washed it in antiseptic.'

That hardly mattered now. It wouldn't after its long immersion, bear prints, if it had ever done so. But the appearance of the necklace surprised him. It wasn't, as had been believed, composed of links, but was a solid collar of grey metal from which almost all the gilding had disappeared, and it was in the shape of a snake twisted into a circle, the snake's head passing, when the necklace was fastened, through a slot above its tail. Now he could see the answer to something that had long puzzled him. This

148

was no chain that might snap when strained but a perfect strangler's weapon. All Hathall's accomplice had had to do was stand behind her victim, grasp the snake's head and pull ...

But how could it have got into the disused cesspit? The metal cover, for use when the pit was emptied, had been buried under a layer of earth and so overgrown with grass that Wexford's men hadn't even guessed it might be there. He phoned Mark Somerset.

'I think I can tell you how it got there,' said Somerset. 'When the main drainage came through, my father, for the sake of economy, only had what's called the "black water" linked on to it. The "grey water" – that is, the waste from the bath, the hand basin and the kitchen sink – went on passing into the cesspit. Bury Cottage is on a bit of a slope, so he knew it wouldn't flood but would just soak away.'

'D'you mean someone could have simply dropped the thing down the sink plughole?'

'I don't see why not. If "someone" ran the taps hard, it'd get washed down.'

'Thank you, Mr Somerset. That's very helpful. By the way, I'd like to – er, express my sympathy for you in the loss of your wife.'

Was it his imagination, or did Somerset sound for the first time ill-at-ease? 'Well, yes, thanks,' he muttered and he rang off abruptly.

When he had the necklace examined by laboratory experts, he asked for an appointment with the chief constable. This was granted for the following Friday afternoon and by two o'clock on that day he was in Griswold's own house, a tarted-up, unfarm-like farmhouse in a village called Millerton between Myringham and Sewingbury. It was known as Hightrees Farm but Wexford privately called it Millerton-*Les-Deux-Eglises*.

'What makes you think this is the weapon?' were Griswold's opening words.

'I feel it's the only type of necklace which could have been used, sir. A chain would have snapped. The lab boys say the gilt which remains on it is similar to the specimens of gilding taken from Angela Hathall's neck. Of course they can't be sure.'

'But I suppose they've got a "feeling"? Have you got any reason to believe that necklace hadn't been there for twenty years?'

Wexford knew better than to mention his feelings again. 'No, but I might have if I could talk to Hathall.'

'He wasn't there when she was killed,' said Griswold, his mouth turning down and his eyes growing hard.

'His girl-friend was.'

'Where? When? I am supposed to be the chief constable of Mid-Sussex where this murder was committed. Why am I not told if the identity of some female accomplice has been discovered?'

'I haven't exactly ...'

'Reg,' said Griswold in a voice that had begun to tremble with anger, 'have you got any more evidence of Robert Hathall's complicity in this than you had fourteen months ago? Have you got one concrete piece of evidence? I asked you that before and I'm asking you again. *Have you?'*

Wexford hesitated. He couldn't reveal that he had had Hathall followed, still less that Chief Superintendent Howard Fortune, his own nephew, had seen him with a woman. What evidence of homicide lay in Hathall's economy or the sale of his car? What guilt was evinced by the man's living in North-west London or his having been seen to catch a London bus? There was the South American thing, of course ... Grimly, Wexford faced just what that amounted to. Nothing. As far as he could prove, Hathall had been offered no job in South America, hadn't even bought a brochure about South America, let alone an air ticket. He had merely been seen to go into a travel agency, and seen by a man with a criminal record.

'No, sir.'

'Then the situation is unchanged. Totally unchanged. Remember that.'

14

Ginge had done as he was told, and on Friday, 8 November, a report arrived from him stating that he had been at his observation post in the pub each evening and on two of those evenings, the Monday and the Wednesday, Hathall had appeared at West End Green just before seven and had caught the 28 bus. That, at any rate, was something. There should have been another report on the Monday. Instead, the unheard-of happened and Ginge phoned. He was phoning from a call-box and he had, he told Wexford, plenty of two and ten pence pieces, and he knew a gentleman like the chief inspector would reimburse him.

'Give me the number and I'll call you myself.' For God's sake, how much of this was he supposed to stand out of his own pocket? Let the ratepayers fork out. Ginge picked up the receiver before the bell had rung twice. 'It has to be good, Ginge, to get you to the phone.'

'I reckon it's bleeding good,' said Ginge cockily. 'I seen him with a bird, that's what.'

The same climactic exultation is never reached twice. Wexford had heard those words – or words having the same meaning – before, and this time he didn't go off into flights about the Lord delivering Hathall into his hands. Instead he asked when and where.

'You know all that about me stationing myself in that pub and watching the bleeding bus stop? Well, I thought to myself there was no harm doing it again Sunday.' Make sure he got seven days' worth of cash and Demon Kings, thought Wexford. 'So I was in there Sunday dinnertime – that is, yesterday like – when I seen him. About one it was and pissing down with rain. He'd got a mac on and his umbrella up. He didn't stop to catch no bus but went right on walking down West End Lane. Well, I never give a bleeding thought to following him. I seen him go by and that was all. But I'd got to thinking I'd better be off to my own dinner – on account of the wife likes it on the table one-thirty sharp – so down I goes to the station.'

'Which station?'

'Wes' Haamsted Stesh'n', said Ginge with a very lifelike imitation of a West Indian bus conductor. He chortled at his own wit. 'When I get there I'm putting a five-pee bit in the machine, on account of

153

its being only one stop to Kilburn, when I see the party standing by the bleeding barrier. He'd got his back to me, thank Gawd, so I nips over to the bookstall and has a look at the girlie mags of what they've got a very choice selection. Well, bearing in mind my duty to you, Mr Wexford, I see my train come in but I don't run down the bleeding steps to catch it. I wait. And up the steps comes about twenty people. I never dared turn round, not wanting my other eye poked, but when I think the coast's clear, I has a bit of a shufty and he'd gone.

'I nips back into West End Lane like a shot and the rain's coming down like stair rods. But up ahead, on his way home, is bleeding Hathall with this bird. Walking very close, they was, under his bleeding umbrella, and the bird's wearing one of them see-through plastic macs with the hood up. I couldn't see no more of her, barring she was wearing a long skirt all trailing in the bleeding wet. So I went off home then and got a bleeding mouthful from the wife for being late for my dinner.'

'Virtue is its own reward, Ginge.'

'I don't know about that,' said Ginge, 'but you'll be wanting to know what my wages and the Demon Kings came to, and the bill's fifteen pound sixty-three. Terrible, the cost of bleeding living, isn't it?'

It wouldn't be necessary, Wexford decided as he put the phone down, to think any longer of ways and means of following a man on a bus. For this man had taken this bus only as far as West Hampstead station, had walked instead this Sunday because he had an umbrella and umbrellas are always a problem on buses. It must be possible now to catch Hathall and his woman together and follow them to Dartmeet Avenue.

'I've got a fortnight's holiday owing to me,' he said to his wife.

'You've got about three months' holiday owing to you with what's mounted up over the years.'

'I'm going to take a bit of it now. Next week, say.'

'What, in November? Then we'll have to go somewhere warm. They say Malta's very nice in November.'

'Chelsea's very nice in November too, and that's where we're going.'

The first thing to do on the first day of his 'holiday' was to familiarize himself with a so far unknown bit of London's geography. Friday, 22 November, was a fine sunny day, June in appearance if January in temperature. How better to get to West Hampstead than on the 28 bus? Howard had told him that its route passed across the King's Road on its way to Wandsworth Bridge, so it wasn't a long walk from Teresa Street to the nearest stop. The bus went up through Fulham into West Kensington, an area he remembered from the time he had helped Howard on that former case, and he noticed to his satisfaction certain familiar landmarks. But soon he was in unknown territory and very varied and vast territory it was. The immense size of London always surprised him. He had had no inkling when he had interrupted Ginge's recitation of the stops on this route of how long the list would have been. Naively, he had supposed that Ginge would have named no more than two or three further places before the terminus, whereas in fact there would have been a dozen. As the conductor sang out, 'Church Street', 'Notting Hill Gate', 'Pembridge Road', he felt a growing relief that Hathall had merely caught the bus to West Hampstead station.

This station was reached at last after about three-quarters of an hour. The bus went on over a bridge above railway lines and past two more stations on the opposite side, West End Lane and another West Hampstead on some suburban line. It had been climbing ever since it left Kilburn and it went on climbing up narrow winding West End Lane till it reached West End Green. Wexford got off. The air was fresh here, not only fresh in comparison to that of Chelsea, but nearly as diesel-free as in Kingsmarkham. Surreptitiously, he consulted his guide. Dartmeet Avenue lay about a quarter of a mile to the east, and he was a little puzzled by this. Surely Hathall could have walked to West Hampstead station in five minutes and walked by the back doubles. Why catch a bus? Still, Ginge had seen him do it. Maybe he merely disliked walking.

Wexford found Dartmeet Avenue with ease. It was a hilly street like most of the streets round here and lined with fine tall houses built mostly of red brick, but some had been modernized and faced with stucco, their sash windows replaced by sheets of plain plate glass. Tall trees, now almost leafless, towered above roofs and pointed gables, and there were mature unpollarded trees growing in the pavements. Number 62 had a front garden that was all shrubbery and weeds. Three black plastic dustbins with 62 painted on their sides in whitewash stood in the side entrance. Wexford noted the phonebox where Ginge had kept his vigils and decided which of the bay windows must be Hathall's. Could anything be gained by calling on the landlord? He concluded that nothing could. The man would be bound to tell Hathall someone had been enquiring about him, would describe that someone, and then the fat would be in the fire. He turned away and walked slowly back to West End Green, looking about him as he did so for such nooks, crannies and convenient trees as might afford him shelter if he dared tail Hathall himself. Night closed in early now, the evenings were long and dark, and in a car ...

The 28 bus sailed down Fortune Green Road as he reached the stop. It was a good frequent service. Wexford wondered, as he settled himself behind the driver, if Robert Hathall had ever sat on that very seat and looked out through this window upon the three stations and the radiating railway lines. Such ruminations verged on the obsessional, though, and that he must avoid. But it was impossible to refrain from wondering afresh why Hathall had caught the bus at all just to reach this point. The woman, when she came to Hathall's home, came by train. Perhaps Hathall didn't like the Tube train, got sick of travelling to work by Tube, so that when he went to her home, he preferred the relaxation of a bus ride.

It took about ten minutes to get to Kilburn. Ginge, who was as sure to be found in the Countess of Castlemaine at noon as the sun is to rise at daybreak or the sound of thunder to follow the sight of lightning, was hunched on his bar stool. He was nursing a half of bitter but when he saw his patron he pushed the tankard away from him, the way a man leaves his spoon in his half-consumed soup when his steak arrives. Wexford ordered a Demon King by name and without description of its ingredients. The barman understood.

'He's got you on your toes, this bleeder, hasn't he?' Ginge moved to an alcove table. 'Always popping up to the Smoke, you are. You don't want to let it get on top of you. Once let a thing like that get a hold on you and you could end up in a bleeding bin.'

'Don't be so daft,' said Wexford, whose own wife had said much the same thing to him that morning, though in more refined terms. 'It won't be for much longer, anyway. This coming week ought to see an end of it. Now what I want you to do ...'

'It won't be for *no* longer, Mr Wexford.' Ginge spoke with a kind of shrinking determination. 'You put me on this to spot him with a bird and I've spotted him with a bird. The rest's up to you.'

'Ginge,' Wexford began cajolingly, 'just to watch the station next week while I watch the house.'

'No,' said Ginge.

'You're a coward.'

'Cowardness,' said Ginge, exhibiting his usual difficulty in making his command of the spoken language match up to his mastery of the written,' 'don't come into it.' He hesitated and said with what might have been modesty or shame, 'I've got a job.'

Wexford almost gasped. 'A *job*?' In former days this monosyllable had exclusively been employed by Ginge and his brother to denote a criminal exercise. 'You mean you've got paid work?'

'Not me. Not exactly.' Ginge contemplated his Demon King rather sadly and, lifting his glass, he sipped from it delicately and with a kind of nostalgia. *Sit transit gloria mundi* or it had been good while it lasted. 'The wife has. Bleeding barmaid. Evenings and Sunday dinnertimes.' He looked slightly embarrassed. 'Don't know what's got into her.'

'What I don't know is why it stops you working for me.'

'Anyone'd think,' said Ginge, 'you'd never had no bleeding family of your own. Someone's got to stay home and mind the kids, haven't they?'

Wexford managed to delay his outburst of mirth until he was out on the pavement. Laughter did him good, cleansing him of the feverish baulked feeling Ginge's refusal to cooperate further had at first brought him. He could manage on his own now, he thought as once more he boarded the 28 bus, and manage for the future in his car. From his car he could watch West Hampstead station on Sunday. With luck, Hathall would meet the woman there as he had done on the previous Sunday, and once the woman was found, what would it matter that Hathall knew he had been followed? Who would reproach him for breaking the rules when his disobedience had resulted in that success?

But Hathall didn't meet the woman on Sunday, and as the week wore on Wexford wondered at the man's elusiveness. He stationed himself in Dartmeet Avenue every evening but he never saw Hathall and he only once saw evidence of occupancy of the room with the bay window. On the Monday, the Tuesday and the Wednesday he was there before six and he saw three people enter the house between six and seven. No sign of Hathall. For some reason, the traffic was particularly heavy on the Thursday evening. It was six-fifteen before he got to Dartmeet Avenue. Rain was falling steadily and the long hilly street was black and glittering with here and there on its surface the gilt glare of reflected lamplight. The place was deserted but for a cat which snaked from between the dustbins and vanished through a fissure in the garden wall. A light was on in a downstairs room and a feebler glow showed through the fanlight above the front door. Hathall's window was dark, but as Wexford put on the handbrake and switched off the ignition, the bay window suddenly became a brilliant yellow cube. Hathall was in, had arrived home perhaps a minute before Wexford's own arrival. For a few seconds the window blazed, then curtains were drawn across it by an invisible hand until all that could be seen were thin perpendicular lines of light like phosphorescent threads gleaming on the dim wet façade.

The excitement this sight had kindled in him cooled as an hour, two hours, went by and Hathall didn't appear. At half past nine a little elderly man emerged, routed out the cat from among the sodden weeds and carried it back into the house. As the front door closed on him, the light that rimmed Hathall's curtains went out. That alerted Wexford and he started to move the car to a less conspicuous position, but the front door remained closed, the window remained dark, and he realized that Hathall had retired early to bed.

Having brought Dora to London for a holiday, he remembered his duty to her and squired her about the West End shopping centres in the daytime. But Denise was so much more adept at doing this than he that on the Friday he deserted his wife and his nephew's wife for a less attractive woman who was no longer a wife at all.

The first thing he saw when he came to Eileen Hathall's house was her ex-husband's car parked on the garage drive, the car which Ginge said had long ago been sold. Had Ginge made a mistake about that? He drove on till he came to a call-box where he phoned Marcus Flower. Yes, Mr Hathall was in, said the voice of a Jane or a Julie or a Linda. If he would just hold the line ... Instead of holding the line, he put the receiver back and within five minutes he was in Eileen Hathall's arid living room, sitting on a cushionless chair under the Spanish gypsy.

'He gave his car to Rosemary,' she said in answer to his question. 'She sees him sometimes at her gran's, and when she said she'd passed her test he gave her his car. He won't need it where he's going, will he?'

'Where is he going, Mrs Hathall?'

'Brazil'. She spat out the rough r and the sibilant as if the word were not the name of a country but of some loathsome reptile. Wexford felt a chill, a sudden anticipation that something bad was coming. It came. 'He's all fixed up,' she said, 'to go the day before Christmas Eve.'

In less than a month ...

'Has he got a job there?' he said steadily.

'A very good position with a firm of international accountants.' There was something pathetic about the pride she took in saying it. The man hated her, had humiliated her, would probably never see her again, yet for all that, she was bitterly proud of what he had achieved. 'You wouldn't believe the money he's getting. He told Rosemary and she told me. They're paying me from London, deducting what I get before it goes to him. He'll still have thousands and thousands a year to live on. And they're paying his fare, fixing it all up, got a house there waiting for him. He hasn't had to do a thing.'

Should he tell her Hathall wouldn't be going alone, wouldn't live in that house alone? She had grown stouter in the past year, her thick body – all bulges where there should be none – stuffed into salmon-pink wool. And she was permanently flushed as if she ran an endless race. Perhaps she did. A race to keep up with her daughter, keep pace with rage and leave the quiet dullness of misery behind. While he was hesitating, she said, 'Why d'you want to know? You think he killed that woman, don't you?'

'Do *you*?' he said boldly.

If she had been struck across the face her skin couldn't have crimsoned more deeply. It looked like flogged skin about to split and bleed. 'I wish he had!' she said on a harsh gasp, and she put up her hand, not to cover her eyes as he had at first thought, but her trembling mouth.

He drove back to London, to a fruitless Friday night vigil, an empty Saturday, a Sunday that might – just might – bring him what he desired.

1 December, and once more pouring with rain. But this was no bad thing. It would clear the streets and make the chance of Hathall's peering into a suspicious-looking car less likely. By half past twelve he had parked as nearly opposite the station as he dared, for it wasn't only the chance of being spotted by Hathall that worried him, but also the risk of obstructing this narrow bottleneck. Rain drummed hard on the car roof, streamed down the gutter between the kerb and the yellow painted line. But this rain was so heavy that, as it washed over the windscreen, it didn't obscure his view but had only a distorting effect as if there were a fault in the glass. He could see the station entrance quite clearly and about a hundred yards of West End Lane where it humped over the railway lines. Trains rattled unseen beneath him, 159 and 28 buses climbed and descended the hill. There were few people about and yet it seemed as if a whole population were travelling, proceeding from unknown homes to unknown destinations through the wet pallid gloom of this winter Sunday. The hands of the dashboard

clock crawled slowly through and past the third quarter after twelve.

By now he was so used to waiting, resigned to sitting on watch like a man who stalked some wary cunning animal, that he felt a jolt of shock which was almost disbelief when at ten to one he saw Hathall's figure in the distance. The glass played tricks with him. He was like someone in a hall of mirrors, first a skeletal giant, then a fat dwarf, but a single sweep of the windscreen wipers brought him suddenly into clear focus. His umbrella up, he was walking swiftly towards the station – fortunately, on the opposite side of the road. He passed the car without turning his head, and outside the station he stopped, snapped the umbrella shut and open, shut, open and shut, to shake off the water drops. Then he disappeared into the entrance.

Wexford was in a dilemma. Was he meeting someone or travelling himself? In daylight, even in this rain, he dared not leave the car. A red train scuttled under the road and came to a stop. He held his breath. The first people to get off the train began to come out on to the pavement. One man put a newspaper over his head and ran, a little knot of women fluttered, struggling with umbrellas that wouldn't open. Three opened simultaneously, a red one, a blue one and an orange pagoda, blossoming suddenly in the greyness like flowers. When they had lifted and danced off, what their brilliant circles had hidden was revealed – a couple with their backs to the street, a couple who stood close together but not touching each other while the man opened a black umbrella and enclosed them under its canopy.

She wore blue jeans and over them a white raincoat, the hood of which was up. Wexford hadn't been able to catch a glimpse of her face. They had set off as if they meant to walk it, but a taxi came splashing down with its For Hire light glowing orange like a cigarette end. Hathall hailed it and it bore them off northwards. Please God, thought Wexford, let it take them home and not to some restaurant. He knew he hadn't a hope of tailing a London taxi-driver, and the cab had vanished before he was out into West End Lane and off.

And the journey up the hill was maddeningly slow. He was bogged down behind a 159 bus – a bus that wasn't red but painted all over with an advertisement for Dinky Toys which reminded him of Kidd's at Toxborough – nearly ten minutes had passed before he drew up in front of the house in Dartmeet Avenue. The taxi had gone, but Hathall's light was on. Of course he'd have to put the light on at midday on such a day as this. Wondering with interest rather than fear if Hathall would hit him too, he went up the path and examined the bells. There were no names by the bell-pushes, just floor numbers. He pressed the first-floor bell and waited. It was possible Hathall wouldn't come down, would just refuse to answer it. In that case, he'd find someone else to let him in and he'd hammer on Hathall's room door.

This turned out to be unnecessary. Above his head

the window opened and, stepping back, he looked up into Hathall's face. For a moment neither of them spoke. The rain dashed between them and they stared at each other through it while a variety of emotions crossed Hathall's features – astonishment, anger, cautiousness, but not, Wexford thought, fear. And all were succeeded by what looked strangely like satisfaction. But before he could speculate as to what this might mean, Hathall said coldly:

'I'll come down and let you in.'

Within fifteen seconds he had done so. He closed the door quietly, saying nothing, and pointed to the stairs. Wexford had never seen him so calm and suave. He seemed entirely relaxed. He looked younger and he looked triumphant.

'I should like you to introduce me to the lady you brought here in a taxi.'

Hathall didn't demur. He didn't speak. As they went up the stairs Wexford thought, has he hidden her? Sent her to some bathroom or up on to the top floor? His room door was on the latch and he pushed it open, allowing the chief inspector to precede him. Wexford, walked in. The first thing he saw was her raincoat, spread out to dry over a chair back.

At first he didn't see her. The room was very small, no more than twelve feet by ten, and furnished as such places always are. There was a wardrobe that looked as if it had been manufactured round about the time of the Battle of Mons, a narrow bed with an Indian cotton cover, some wooden-armed chairs that are euphemistically known as 'fireside', and pictures that had doubtless been painted by some relative of the landlord's. The light came from a dust-coated plastic sphere suspended from the pock-marked ceiling.

A canvas screen, canvas-coloured and hideous, shut off one corner of the room. Behind it, presumably, was a sink, for when Hathall gave a cautionary cough, she pushed it aside and came out, drying her hands on a tea towel. It wasn't a pretty face, just a very young one, heavy-featured, tough and confident. Thick black hair fell to her shoulders and her eyebrows were heavy and black like a man's. She wore a teeshirt with a cardigan over it, Wexford had seen that face somewhere before, and he was wondering where when Hathall said:

'This is the "lady" you wanted to meet.' His triumph had changed to frank amusement and he was almost laughing. 'May I present my daughter, Rosemary?'

15

It was a long time since Wexford had experienced such an anticlimax. Coping with awkward situations wasn't usually a problem with him, but the shock of what Hathall had just said – combined with his realization that his own disobedience was now known – stunned him into silence. The girl didn't speak either after she had said a curt hello, but retreated behind the screen where she could be heard filling a kettle.

Hathall, who had been so withdrawn and aloof when Wexford first arrived, seemed to be getting the maximum possible enjoyment from his adversary's dismay. 'What's this visit in aid of?' he asked. 'Just looking up old acquaintances?'

In for a penny, in for a pound, thought Wexford,

echoing Miss Marcovitch. 'I understand you're going to Brazil,' he said. 'Alone?'

'Can one go alone? There'll be about three hundred other people in the aircraft.' Wexford smarted under that one and Hathall saw him smart. 'I hoped Rosemary might go with me, but her school is here. Perhaps she'll join me in a few years' time.'

That fetched the girl out. She picked up her raincoat, hung it on a hanger and said, 'I haven't even been to Europe yet. I'm not burying myself in Brazil.'

Hathall shrugged at this typical sample of his family's ungraciousness, and said as brusquely, 'Satisfied?'

'I have to be, don't I, Mr Hathall?'

Was it his daughter's presence that kept his anger in check? He was almost mild, only a trace of his usual resentful querulousness sounding in his voice when he said, 'Well, if you'll excuse us, Rosemary and I have to get ourselves some lunch which isn't the easiest thing in the world in this little hole. I'll see you out.'

He closed the door instead of leaving it on the latch. It was dark and quiet on the landing. Wexford waited for the explosion of rage but it didn't come, and he was conscious only of the man's eyes. They were the same height and their eyes met on a level. Briefly, Hathall's showed white and staring around hard black irises in which that curious red spark glittered. They were at the head of the steep flight of stairs, and as Wexford turned to descend them, he was aware of a movement behind him, of Hathall's splayed hand rising. He grasped the banister and swung down a couple of steps. Then he made himself walk down slowly and steadily. Hathall didn't move, but when Wexford reached the bottom and looked back, he saw the raised hand lifted higher and the fingers closed in a solemn and somehow portentous gesture of farewell.

'He was going to push me down those stairs,' Wexford said to Howard. 'And I wouldn't have had much redress. He could have said I'd forced my way into his room. God, what a mess I've made of things! He's bound to put in another of his complaints and I could lose my job.'

'Not without a pretty full enquiry, and I don't think Hathall would want to appear at any enquiry.' Howard threw the Sunday paper he had been reading on to the floor and turned his thin bony face, his ice-blue penetrating eyes, towards his uncle. 'It wasn't his daughter all the time, Reg.'

'Wasn't it? I know you saw this woman with short fair hair, but can you be sure it was Hathall you saw her with?'

'I'm sure.'

'You saw him once,' Wexford persisted. 'You saw him twenty yards off for about ten seconds from a car *you were driving*. If you had to go into court and swear that the man you saw outside Marcus Flower was the same man you saw in the garden of Bury Cottage, would you swear? If a man's life depended on it, would you?'

'Capital punishment is no longer with us, Reg.'

'No, and neither you nor I – unlike many of our

calling – would wish to see it back. But if it were with us, then would you?'

Howard hesitated. Wexford saw that hesitation and he felt tiredness creep through his body like a depressant drug. Even a shred of doubt could dispel what little hope he now had left.

At last, 'No, I wouldn't,' Howard said flatly.

'I see.'

'Wait a minute, Reg. I'm not sure nowadays if I could ever swear to a man's identity if my swearing to it might lead to his death. You're pressing me too hard. But I'm sure beyond a reasonable doubt, and I'll still say to you, yes, I saw Robert Hathall. I saw him outside the offices of Marcus Flower in Half Moon Street with a fair-haired woman.'

Wexford sighed. What difference did it make, after all? By his own blundering of that day he had put an end to all hope of following Hathall. Howard mistook his silence for doubt and said, 'If he isn't with her, where does he go all those evenings he's out? Where did he go on that bus?'

'Oh, I still believe he's with her. The daughter just goes there sometimes on Sundays. But what good does that do me? I can't follow him on a bus. He'll be looking for me now.'

'He'll think, you know, that seeing him with his daughter will put you off.'

'Maybe. Maybe he'll get reckless. So what? I can't conceal myself in a doorway and leap on a bus after him. Either the bus would go before I got on or he'd turn round and see me. Even if I got on without his seeing me ...'

'Then someone else must do it,' said Howard firmly.

'Easy to say. My chief constable says no, and you won't cross swords with my chief constable by letting me have one of your blokes.'

'That's true, I won't.'

'Then we may as well give over talking about it. I'll go back to Kingsmarkham and face the music – a bloody great symphony in Griswold sharp major – and Hathall can go to the sunny tropics.'

Howard got up and laid a hand on his shoulder. 'I will do it,' he said.

The awe had gone long ago, giving way to love and comradeship. But that 'I will do it', spoken so lightly and pleasantly, brought back all the old humiliation and envy and awareness of the other's advantages. Wexford felt a hot dark flush suffuse his face. '*You*?' he said roughly, 'you yourself? You must be joking. You take rank over me, remember?'

'Don't be such a snob. What if I do? I'd like to do it. It'd be fun. I haven't done anything like that for years and years.'

'Would you really do that for me, Howard? What about your own work?'

'If I'm the god you make me out to be, don't you think I have some say in the hours I work? Of course I shan't be able to do it every night. There'll be the usual crises that come up from time to time and I'll have to stay late. But Kenbourne Vale won't degenerate into a sort of twentieth-century Bridewell just because I pop up to West Hampstead every so often.'

So on the following evening Chief Superintendent Howard Fortune left his office at a quarter to six and was at West End Green on the hour. He waited until half past seven. When his quarry didn't come, he made his way along Dartmeet Avenue and observed that there was no light on in the window his uncle had told him was Hathall's.

'I wonder if he's going to her straight from work?'

'Let's hope he's not going to make a habit of that. It'll be almost impossible to follow him in the rush hour. When does he give up this job of his?'

'God knows,' said Wexford, 'but he leaves for Brazil in precisely three weeks.'

One of those crises at which he had hinted prevented Howard from tailing Hathall on the following night, but he was free on the Wednesday and, changing his tactics, he got to Half Moon Street by five o'clock. An hour later, in Teresa Street, he told his uncle what had happened.

'The first person to come out of Marcus Flower was a seedy-looking guy with a toothbrush moustache. He had a girl with him and they went off in a Jaguar.'

'That'd be Jason Marcus and his betrothed,' said Wexford.

'Then two more girls and then – Hathall. I *was* right, Reg. It's the same man.'

'I shouldn't have doubted you.'

Howard shrugged. 'He got into the Tube and I lost him. But he wasn't going home. I know that.'

'How can you know?'

'If he'd been going home he'd have walked to Green Park station, gone one stop on the Piccadilly Line to Piccadilly Circus or on the Victoria Line to Oxford Circus and changed on to the Bakerloo. He'd have walked south. But he walked north, and at first I thought he was going to get a bus home. But he went to Bond Street station. You'd never go to Bond Street if you meant to go to North-west London. Bond Street's only on the Central Line until the Fleet Line opens.'

'And the Central Line goes where?'

'Due east and due west. I followed him into the station but – well, you've seen our rush hours, Reg. I was a good dozen people behind him in the ticket queue. The thing was I had to be so damn careful he didn't get a look at me. He went down the escalator to the westbound platform – and I lost him.' Howard said apologetically, 'There were about five hundred people on the platform. I got stuck and I couldn't move. But it's proved one thing. D'you see what I mean?'

'I think so. We have to find where the westbound Central Line route crosses the 28 bus route, and somewhere in that area lives our unknown woman.'

'I can tell you where that is straight off. The westbound Central Line route goes Bond Street, Marble Arch, Lancaster Gate, Queensway, Notting Hill Gate, Holland Park, Shepherd's Bush, and so on. The south-bound 28 route goes Golders Green, West Hampstead, Kilburn, Kilburn Park, Great

Western Road, Pembridge Road, Notting Hill Gate, Church Street, on through Kensington and Fulham to here and ultimately to Wandsworth. So it has to be Notting Hill. She lives, along with half the roving population of London, somewhere in Notting Hill. Small progress, but better than nothing. Have you made any?'

Wexford, on tenterhooks for two days, had phoned Burden, expecting to hear that Griswold was out for his blood. But nothing was further from the truth. The chief constable had been 'buzzing around' Kingsmarkham, as Burden put it, tearing between there and Myringham where there was some consternation over a missing woman. But he had been in an excellent frame of mind, had asked where Wexford had gone for his holiday, and on being told London ('For the theatres and museums, you know, sir,' Burden had said) had asked facetiously why the chief inspector hadn't sent him a picture postcard of New Scotland Yard.

'Then Hathall hasn't complained,' said Howard thoughtfully.

'Doesn't look like it. If I were to be optimistic, I'd say he thinks it safer not to draw attention to himself.'

But it was 3 December ... Twenty days to go. Dora had dragged her husband round the stores, doing the last of her Christmas shopping. He had carried her parcels, agreed that this was just the thing for Sheila and that was exactly what Sylvia's elder boy wanted, but all the time he was thinking, twenty days, twenty days ... This year Christmas for him would be the season of Robert Hathall's getaway.

Howard seemed to read his thoughts. He was eating one of those enormous meals he consumed without putting on a pound. Taking a second helping of *charlotte russe*, he said, 'If only we could get him on something.'

'What d'you mean?

'I don't know. Some little thing you could hold him on that would stop him leaving the country. Like shoplifting, say, or travelling on the Tube without a ticket.'

'He seems to be an honest man,' said Wexford bitterly, 'if you can call a murderer honest.'

His nephew scraped the dessert bowl. 'I suppose he *is* honest?'

'As far as I know, he is. Mr Butler would have told me if there's been a smell of dishonesty about him.'

'I daresay. Hathall was all right for money in those days. But he wasn't all right for money when he got married to Angela, was he? Yet, in spite of their having only fifteen pounds a week to live on, they started doing all right. You told me Somerset had seen them on a shopping spree and then dining at some expensive place. Where did that money come from, Reg?'

Pouring himself a glass of Chablis, Wexford said, 'I've wondered about that. But I've never come to any conclusion. It didn't seem relevant.'

'Everything's relevant in a murder case.'

'True.' Wexford was too grateful to his nephew

to react huffily at this small admonition. 'I suppose I reckoned that if a man's always been honest he doesn't suddenly become dishonest in middle age.'

'That depends on the man. This man suddenly became an unfaithful husband in middle age. In fact, although he'd been monogamous since puberty, he seems to have turned into a positive womanizer in middle age. And he became a murderer. I don't suppose you're saying he killed anyone before, are you?' Howard pushed away his plate and started on the gruyère. 'There's one factor in all this I don't think you've taken into sufficient account. One personality.'

'Angela?'

'Angela. It was when he met her that he changed. Some would say she'd corrupted him. This is an outside chance – a very way-out idea altogether – but Angela had been up to a little fraud on her own, one you know about, possibly others you don't. Suppose she encouraged him into some sort of dishonesty?'

'Your saying that reminds me of something Mr Butler said. He said he overheard Angela tell his partner, Paul Craig, that he was in a good position to fiddle his income tax.'

'There you are then. They must have got that money from somewhere. It didn't grow on trees like the "miracle" plums.'

'There hasn't been a hint of anything,' said Wexford. 'It would have to be at Kidd's. Aveney didn't drop so much as a hint.'

'But you weren't asking him about money. You were asking him about women.' Howard got up from the table and pushed aside his chair. 'Let's go and join the ladies. If I were you I'd take a little trip to Toxborough tomorrow.'

16

The rectangular white box set on green lawns, the screen of saplings, leafless and pathetic in December, and inside, the warm cellulose smell and the turbanned women painting dolls to the theme music from *Doctor Zhivago*. Mr Aveney conducted Wexford through the workshops to the office of the personnel manager, talking the while in a shocked and rather indignant way.

'Cooking the books? We've never had anything like that here.'

'I'm not saying you have, Mr Aveney. I'm working in the dark,' said Wexford. 'Have you ever heard of the old pay-roll fiddle?'

'Well, yes, I *have*. It used to be done a lot in the forces. No one'd get away with it here.'

'Let's see, shall we?'

The personnel manager, a vague young man with fair bristly hair, was introduced as John Oldbury. His office was very untidy and he seemed somewhat distraught as if he had been caught in the middle of searching for something he knew he would never find. 'Messing about with the wages, d'you mean?' he said.

'Suppose you tell me how you work with the accountant to manage the pay-roll.'

Oldbury looked distractedly at Aveney, and Aveney nodded, giving an infinitesimal shrug. The personnel manager sat down heavily and pushed his fingers through his unruly hair. 'I'm not very good at explaining things,' he began. 'But I'll try. It's like this: when we get a new worker I sort of tell the accountant details about her and he works them out for her wages. No, I'll have to be more explicit. Say we take on a – well, we'll call her Joan Smith, Mrs Joan Smith.' Oldbury, thought Wexford, was as unimaginative as he was inarticulate. 'I tell the accountant her name and her address – say ...'

Seeing his total defeat, Wexford said, 'Twenty-four Gordon Road, Toxborough.'

'Oh, fine!' The personnel manager beamed his admiration. 'I tell him Mrs Joan Smith, of whatever-it-is Gordon Road, Toxborough ...'

'Tell him by what means? Phone? A chit?'

'Well, either. Of course I keep a record. I haven't,' said Oldbury unnecessarily, 'got a very good memory. I tell him her name and her address and when she's starting and her hours and whatever, and he feeds all that into the computer and Bob's your uncle. And after that I do it every week for her overtime and – and whatever.'

'And when she leaves you tell him that too?'

'Oh, sure.'

'They're always leaving. Chop and change, it's everlasting,' said Aveney.

'They're all paid in weekly wage packets?'

'Not all,' said Oldbury. 'You see, some of our ladies don't use their wages for – well, housekeeping. Their husbands are the – what's the word?'

'Breadwinners?'

'Ah, fine. Breadwinners. The ladies – some of them – keep their wages for holidays and sort of improving their homes and just saving up, I suppose.'

'Yes, I see. But so what?'

'Well,' said Oldbury triumphantly, '*they* don't get wage packets. Their wages are paid into a bank account – more likely the Post Office or a Trustee Savings Bank.'

'And if they are, you tell that to the accountant and he feeds it into his computer?'

'He does, yes.' Oldbury smiled delightedly at the realization he had made himself so clear. 'You're absolutely right. Quick thinking, if I may say so.'

'Not at all,' said Wexford, slightly stupefied by the man's zany charm. 'So the accountant could simply invent a woman and feed a fictitious name and address into the computer? Her wages would go into a bank account which the accountant – or, rather, his female accomplice – could draw on when they chose?'

'That,' said Oldbury severely, 'would be fraud.'

'It would indeed. But, since you keep records, we can easily verify if such a fraud has ever been committed.'

'Of course we can.' The personnel manager beamed again and trotted over to a filing cabinet whose open drawers were stuffed with crumpled documents. 'Nothing easier. We keep records for a whole year after one of our ladies has left us.'

A whole year ... And Hathall had left them eighteen months before. Aveney took him back through the factory where the workers were now being lulled (or stimulated) by the voice of Tom Jones. 'John Oldbury,' he said defensively, 'has got a very good psychology degree and he's marvellous with people.'

'I'm sure. You've both been very good. I apologize for taking up so much of your time.'

The interview had neither proved nor disproved Howard's theory. But since there were no records, what could be done? If the enquiry wasn't a clandestine one, if he had men at his disposal, he could send them round the local Trustee Savings Banks. But it was, and he hadn't. Yet he could see so clearly now how such a thing could have been done; the idea coming in the first place from Angela; the female accomplice brought in to impersonate the women Hathall had invented, and to draw money from the accounts. And then – yes, Hathall growing too fond of his henchwoman so that Angela became jealous. If he was right, everything was explainable, the deliberately contrived solitude of the Hathalls, their cloistral life, the money that enabled them to dine out and Hathall to buy presents for his daughter. And they would all have been in it together – until Angela realized the woman was more than an accomplice to her husband, more than a useful collector of revenues ... What had she done? Broken up the affair and threatened that if it started again, she'd shop them both? That would have meant the end of Hathall's career. That would put paid to his job at Marcus Flower or any future accountancy job. So they had murdered her. They had killed Angela to be together, and knowing Kidd's kept records for only one year, to be safe for ever from the risk of discovery ...

Wexford drove slowly down the drive between the flat green lawns, and at the gateway to the main industrial estate road met another car coming in. Its driver was a uniformed police officer and its other occupant Chief Inspector Jack 'Brock' Lovat, a small snub-nosed man who wore small gold-rimmed glasses. The car slowed and Lovat wound his window down.

'What are you doing here?' Wexford asked.

'My job,' said Lovat simply.

His nickname derived from the fact that he kept three badgers, rescued from the diggers before badger-digging became an offence, in his back garden. And Wexford knew of old that it was useless questioning the head of Myringham CID about anything but this hobby of his. On that subject he was fulsome and enthusiastic. On all others – though he did his work in exemplary fashion – he was almost mute. You got a 'yes' or a 'no' out of him unless you were prepared to talk about setts and plantigrade quadrupeds.

'Since there are no badgers here,' Wexford said sarcastically, 'except possibly clockwork ones, I'll just ask this. Is your visit connected in any way with a man called Robert Hathall?'

'No,' said Lovat. Smiling closely, he waved his hand and told the driver to move on.

But for its new industries, Toxborough would by now have dwindled to a semi-deserted village with an elderly population. Industry had brought life, commerce, roads, ugliness, a community centre, a sports ground and a council estate. This last was traversed by a broad thoroughfare called Maynnot Way, where the concrete stilts of street lamps replaced the trees, and which had been named after the only old house that remained in it, Maynnot Hall. Wexford, who hadn't been this way for ten years when the concrete and the brick had first begun to spread across Toxborough's green fields, knew that somewhere, not too far from here, was a Trustee Savings Bank. At the second junction he turned left into Queen Elizabeth Avenue, and there it was, sandwiched between a betting shop and a place that sold cash-and-carry carpets.

The manager was a stiff pompous man who reacted sharply to Wexford's questions.

'Let you look at our books? Not without a warrant.'

'All right. But tell me this. If payments stop being

made into an account and it's left empty or nearly empty, do you write to the holder and ask him or her if they want it closed?'

'We gave up the practice. If someone's only got fifteen pence in an account he's not going to waste money on a stamp saying he wants the account closed. Nor is he going to spend five pence on a bus fare to collect it. Right?'

'Would you check for me if any accounts held by women have had no payments made into them or withdrawals made from them since – well, last April or May twelvemonth? And if there are any, would you communicate with the holders?'

'Not,' said the manager firmly, 'unless this is an official police matter. I haven't got the staff.'

Neither, thought Wexford as he left the bank, had he. No staff, no funds, no encouragement; and still nothing but his own 'feelings' with which to convince Griswold that this was worth pursuing. Kidd's had a pay-roll, Hathall could have helped himself to money from it by the means of accounts held by fictitious women. Come to that, Kingsmarkham police station had a petty cash box and he, Wexford, could have helped himself out of it. There was about as much ground for suspicion in the latter case as in the former, and that was how the chief constable would see it.

'Another dead end,' he said to his nephew that night. 'But I understand how it all happened now. The Hathalls and the other woman work their fraud for a couple of years. The share-out of the loot takes place at Bury Cottage. Then Hathall gets his new job and there's no longer any need for the pay-roll fiddle. The other woman should fade out of the picture, but she doesn't because Hathall has fallen for her and wants to go on seeing her. You can imagine Angela's fury. It was *her* idea, she planned it, and it's led to this. She tells Hathall to give her up or she'll blow the whole thing, but Hathall can't. He pretends he has and all seems well between him and Angela, to the extent of Angela asking her mother-in-law to stay and cleaning up the cottage to impress her. In the afternoon Angela fetches her rival, perhaps to wind up the whole thing finally. The other woman strangles her as arranged, but leaves that print on the bath.'

'Admirable,' said Howard. 'I'm sure you're right.'

'And much good it does me. I may as well go home tomorrow. You're coming to us for Christmas?'

Howard patted his shoulder as he had done on the day he promised his vigilance. 'Christmas is a fortnight off. I'll keep on watching every free evening I get.'

At any rate, there was no summons from Griswold awaiting him. And nothing much had happened in Kingsmarkham during his absence. The home of the chairman of the rural council had been broken into. Six colour sets had been stolen from the television rental company in the High Street. Burden's son had been accepted by Reading University, subject to satisfactory A Levels. And Nancy Lake's house had been sold for a cool twenty-five thousand pounds. Some said she was moving to London, others that she was going abroad. Sergeant Martin had decorated the police station foyer with paper chains and mobiles of flying angels which the chief constable had ordered removed forthwith as they detracted from the dignity of Mid-Sussex.

'Funny thing Hathall didn't complain, wasn't it?'

'Lucky for you he didn't.' At ease now in his new glasses, Burden looked more severe and puritanical than ever. With a rather exasperated indrawing of breath, he said, 'You must give that up, you know.'

'Must? Little man, little man, *must* is not a word to be addressed to chief inspectors. Time was when you used to call me "sir".'

'And it was you asked me to stop. Remember?'

Wexford laughed. 'Let's go over to the Carousel and have a spot of lunch, and I'll tell you all about what I *must* give up.'

Antonio was delighted to see him back and offered him the speciality of the day – *moussaka*.

'I thought that was Greek.'

'The Greeks,' said Antonio, flinging out his hands, 'got it from us.'

'A reversal of the usual process. How interesting. I may as well have it, Antonio. And steak pie, which you got from *us*, for Mr Burden. Have I got thinner, Mike?'

'You're wasting away.'

'I haven't had a decent meal for a fortnight, what with chasing after that damned Hathall.' Wexford told him about it while they ate. 'Now do you believe?'

'Oh, I don't know. It's mostly in your head, isn't it? My daughter was telling me something the other day she got from school. About Galileo, it was. They made him recant what he'd said about the earth moving round the sun but he wouldn't give it up, and on his death-bed his last words were, "It does move".'

'I've heard it. What are you trying to prove? He was right. The earth does go round the sun. And on *my* death-bed I'll say, "He did do it".' Wexford sighed. It was useless, may as well change the subject … 'I saw old Brock last week. He was as close as ever. Did he find his missing girl?'

'He's digging up Myringham Old Town for her.'

'As missing as that, is she?'

Burden gave Wexford's *moussaka* a suspicious look and a suspicious sniff, and attacked his own steak pie. 'He's pretty sure she's dead and he's arrested her husband.'

'What, for murder?'

'No, not without the body. The bloke's got a record and he's holding him on a shop-breaking charge.'

'Christ!' Wexford exploded. 'Some people have all the luck.'

His eyes met Burden's, and the inspector gave him the kind of look we level at our friends when we begin to doubt their mental equilibrium. And Wexford said no more, breaking the silence only to ask after young John Burden's successes and prospects. But when they rose to go and a beaming Antonio had been congratulated on the cooking,

'When I retire or die, Antonio,' Wexford said, 'will you name a dish after me?'

The Italian crossed himself. 'Nor to speak of such things, but yes, sure I will. *Lasagne* Wexford?'

'*Lasagne Galileo*.' Wexford laughed at the other's puzzlement. 'It sounds more Latin,' he said.

The High Street shops had their windows filled with glitter, and the great cedar outside the Dragon pub had orange and green and scarlet and blue light bulbs in its branches. In the toyshop window a *papier mâché* and cotton wool Santa Claus nodded and smiled and gyrated at an audience of small children who pressed their noses to the glass.

'Twelve more shopping days to Christmas,' said Burden. 'Oh, shut up,' Wexford snapped.

17

A grey mist hung over the river, curtaining its opposite bank, shrouding the willows in veils of vapour, making colourless the hills and the leafless woods so that they appeared like a landscape in an out-of-focus monochrome photograph. On this side, the houses of the Old Town slept in the freezing mist, all their windows closed against it, their garden trees utterly still. The only motion was that of water drops falling gently and very slowly from threadlike branches. It was bitterly cold. As Wexford walked down past St Luke's and Church House, it seemed wonderful to him that up there beyond those layers of cloud, miles of icy mist, must be a bright though distant sun. A few more days to the shortest day, the longest night. A few more days to the solstice when the sun would have moved to its extremest limit from this part of the earth. Or as he should put it, he thought, recalling Burden's snippet of pop education from the day before, when the ground on which he stood would have moved to its extremest limit from the sun ...

He saw the police cars and police vans in River Lane before he saw any of the men who had driven them there or any signs of their purpose. They were parked all along the lane, fronting the row of almost derelict houses whose owners had abandoned them and left them to be inhabited intermittently by the desperate homeless. Here and there, where the glass or even the frame of an ancient window had collapsed and gone, the cavity was patched with plastic sheeting. Against other windows hung bedspreads, sacks, rags, torn and soaking brown paper. But there were no squatters here now. Winter and the damp rising from the river had driven them to find other quarters, and the old houses, immeasurably more beautiful even now than any modern terrace, waited in the sour cold for new occupants or new purchasers. They were old but they were also very nearly immortal. No one might destroy them. All that could become of them was a slow disintegration into extreme decay.

An alley led between broken brick walls to the gardens which lay behind them, gardens which had become repositories of rubbish, rat-infested, and which sloped down to the river bank. Wexford made his way down this alley to a point where the wall had caved in, leaving a gap. A young police sergeant, standing just inside and holding a spade in his hand, barred his way and said, 'Sorry, sir. No one's allowed in here.'

'Don't you know me, Hutton?'

The sergeant looked again and, taken aback, said, 'It's Mr Wexford, isn't it? I beg your pardon, sir.'

Wexford said that was quite all right, and where was Chief Inspector Lovat to be found?

'Down where they're digging, sir. On the right-hand side at the bottom.'

'They're digging for this woman's body?'

'Mrs Morag Grey. She and her husband squatted here for a bit the summer before last. Mr Lovat thinks the husband may have buried her in this garden.'

'They lived *here*?' Wexford looked up at the sagging gable, shored up with a baulk of timber. The leprous split plaster had scaled off in places, showing the bundles of wattle the house had been built of four hundred years before. A gaping doorway revealed interior walls which, slimy and running with water, were like those of a cave that the sea invades daily.

'It wouldn't be so bad in summer,' said Hutton by way of apology, 'and they weren't here for more than a couple of months.'

A great tangle of bushes, mud-spattered, under which lay empty cans and sodden newspaper, cut off the end of the garden. Wexford pushed his way through them into a waste land. Four men were digging, and digging more than the three spits deep which is the gardener's rule. Mountains of earth, scattered with chalk splinters, were piled against the river wall. Lovat was sitting on this wall, his coat collar turned up, a thin damp cigarette stuck to his lower lip, watching them inscrutably.

'What makes you think she's here?'

'Got to be somewhere.' Lovat showed no surprise at his arrival but spread another sheet of newspaper on the wall for him to sit down. 'Nasty day,' he said.

'You think the husband killed her?' Wexford knew it was useless asking questions. You had to make statements and wait for Lovat to agree with them or refute them. 'You've got him on a shop-breaking charge. But you've got no body, just a missing woman. Someone must have made you take that seriously, and not Grey himself.'

'Her mother,' said Lovat.

'I see. Everyone thought she'd gone to her mother, and her mother thought she was elsewhere, but she didn't answer mother's letters. Grey's got a record, maybe living with another woman. Told a lot of lies. Am I right?'

'Yes.'

Wexford thought he had done his duty. It was a pity he knew so little about badgers, was even less interested in them than he was in the Grey affair. The icy mist was seeping through his clothes to his spine, chilling his whole body. 'Brock,' he said, 'will you do me a favour?'

Most people when asked that question reply that it all depends on what the favour is. But Lovat had virtues to offset his taciturnity. He took another crumpled cigarette from a damp and crumpled packet. 'Yes,' he said simply.

'You know that guy Hathall I'm always on about? I think he worked a pay-roll fiddle while he was with Kidd's at Toxborough. That's why I was there when we met the other day. But I've no authority to act. I'm pretty sure it was like this ...' Wexford told him what he was pretty sure it was like. 'Would you get someone along to those trustee savings banks and see if you can smell out any false accounts? And quick, Brock, because I've only got ten days.'

Lovat didn't ask why he only had ten days. He wiped his spectacles which the fog had misted and readjusted them on his red snub nose. Without looking at Wexford or showing the least interest, he fixed his eyes on the men and said, 'One way and another I've had a lot to do with digging in my time.'

Wexford made no response. Just at the moment he couldn't summon up much enthusiasm for a League-Against-Cruel-Sports homily. Nor did he repeat his request, which would only have annoyed Lovat, but sat silent in the damp cold listening to the sounds the spades made when they struck chalk, and the soft slump of earth lifted and slung heavily aside. Cans, waterlogged cartons, were lumped on to the growing heaps, to be followed by unearthed rose bushes, their roots scorpion-like and matted with wet soil. Was there a body under there? At any moment a spade might reveal, not a clod of ancient mortar or another mass of brown root, but a white and rotting human hand.

The mist was thickening over the almost stagnant

water. Lovat threw his cigarette end into an oil-scummed puddle. 'Will do,' he said.

It was a relief to get away from the river and its miasma – the miasma that had once been thought of as a breeder of disease – and up into the fashionable part of the Old Town where he had parked his car. He was wiping its misted windscreen when he saw Nancy Lake, and he would have wondered what she was doing there had she not, at that moment, turned into a little baker's shop, famous for its home-baked bread and cakes. More than a year had passed since he had last seen her, and he had almost forgotten the sensation he had felt then, the catching of breath, the faint tremor in the heart. He felt it now as he saw the glass door close on her, the shop's warm orange glow receive her.

Although he was shivering now, his breath like smoke on the cold haze, he waited there for her on the kerb. And when she came out she rewarded him with one of her rich sweet smiles. 'Mr Wexford! There are policemen everywhere down here, but I didn't expect to see you.'

'I'm a policeman too. May I give you a lift back to Kingsmarkham?'

'Thank you, I'm not going back just now.' She wore a chinchilla coat that sparkled with fine drops. The cold which pinched other faces had coloured hers and brightened her eyes. 'But I'll come and sit in your car with you for five minutes, shall I?'

Someone, he thought, ought to invent a way of heating a car while the engine was switched off. But she didn't seem to feel the cold. She leaned towards him with the eagerness and the vitality of a young woman. 'Shall we share a cream cake?'

He shook his head. 'Bad for my figure, I'm afraid.'

'But you've got a lovely figure!'

Knowing that he shouldn't, that this was inviting a renewal of flirtation, he looked into those shining eyes and said, 'You are always saying things to me that no woman has said for half a lifetime.'

She laughed. 'Not always. How can it be "always" when I never see you?' She began to eat a cake. It was the kind of cake no one should attempt to eat without a plate, a fork and a napkin. She managed it with her bare fingers remarkably well, her small red tongue retrieving flecks of cream from her lips. 'I've sold my house,' she said. 'I'm moving out the day before Christmas Eve.'

The day before Christmas Eve ... 'They say that you're going abroad.'

'Do they? They've been saying things about me round here for twenty years and most of it has been a distortion of the truth. Do they say that my dream has come true at last?' She finished her cake, licked her fingers delicately. 'Now I must go. Once – Oh, it seems years ago – I asked you to come and have tea with me.'

'So you did,' he said.

'Will you come? Say – next Friday?' When he nodded, she said, 'And we'll have the last of the miracle jam.'

'I wish you'd tell me why you call it that.'

'I will, I will ...' He held the car door open for her

and she took the hand he held out. 'I'll tell you the story of my life. All shall be made clear. Till Friday, then.'

'Till Friday.' It was absurd, this feeling of excitement. You're old, he told himself sternly. She wants to give you plum jam and tell you the story of her life, that's all you're fit for now. And he watched her walk away until her grey fur had melted into the river mist and was gone.

'I can't follow him on the Tube, Reg. I've tried three times, but each night the crowds get worse with the pre-Christmas rush.'

'I can imagine,' said Wexford, who felt he never wanted to hear the word 'Christmas' again. He was more aware of the season's festive pressures than he had ever been in the past. Was Christmas more christmassy this year than usual? Or was it simply that he saw every card which flopped on to his front door mat, every hint of the coming celebrations, as a threat of failure? There was a bitter irony in the fact that this year they were going to fill the house with more people than ever before, both his daughters, his son-in-law, his two grandsons, Howard and Denise, Burden and his children. And Dora had already begun to put up the decorations. He had to hunch in his chair, the phone on his knees, to avoid prickling his face on the great bunch of holly that hung above his desk. 'That seems to be that then, doesn't it?' he said. 'Give it up, finish. Something may come out of the pay-roll thing. It's my last hope.'

Howard's voice sounded indignant. 'I didn't mean I want to give it up. I only meant I can't do it that way.'

'What other way is there?'

'Why shouldn't I try to tail him from the other end?'

'The other end?'

'Last night after I'd lost him on the Tube, I went up to Dartmeet Avenue. You see, I'd reckoned he may stay all night with her some nights, but he doesn't always stay there. If he did, there'd be no point in his having a place of his own. And he didn't stay last night, Reg. He came home on the last 28 bus. So I thought, why shouldn't I also get on that last bus?'

'I must be getting thick in my old age,' said Wexford, 'but I don't see how that helps.'

'This is now. He'll get on at the stop nearest to her place, won't he? And once I find it I can wait at it the next night from five-thirty onwards. If he comes by bus I can follow him, if he comes by Tube it'll be harder, but there's still a good chance.'

Kilburn Park, Great Western Road, Pembridge Road, Church Street ... Wexford sighed. 'There are dozens of stops,' he said.

'Not in Notting Hill, there aren't. And it has to be Notting Hill, remember. The last 28 bus crosses Notting Hill Gate at ten to eleven. Tomorrow night I'll be waiting for it in Church Street. I've got six more weekday evenings, Reg, six more watching nights to Christmas.'

'You shall have the breast of the turkey,' said

his uncle, 'and the fifty-pence piece from the pudding.'

As he put the phone down, the doorbell rang and he heard the thin reedy voices of young carol singers.

'God rest you merry, gentlemen,
Let nothing you dismay ...'

18

The Monday of the week before Christmas passed and the Tuesday came and there was nothing from Lovat. Very likely he was too busy with the Morag Grey case to make much effort. Her body hadn't been found, and her husband, remanded in custody for a week, was due to appear in court again solely on the shop-breaking charge. Wexford phoned Myringham police station on Tuesday afternoon. If was Mr Lovat's day off, Sergeant Hutton told him, and he wouldn't be found at home as he was attending something called the convention of the Society of Friends of the British Badger.

No word came from Howard. It wasn't awe that stopped Wexford phoning him. You don't harass someone who is doing you the enormous favour of giving up all his free time to gratify your obsession, pursue your chimera. You leave him alone and wait. *Chimera*: Monster, bogy, thing of fanciful conception. That was how the dictionary defined it, Wexford discovered, looking the word up in the solitude of his office. Thing of fanciful conception ... Hathall was flesh and blood all right, but the woman? Only Howard had ever seen her, and Howard wasn't prepared to swear that Hathall – the monster, the bogy – had been her companion. Let nothing you dismay, Wexford told himself. Someone had made that handprint, someone had left those coarse dark hairs on Angela's bedroom floor.

And even if his chances of ever laying hands on her were now remote, growing more remote with each day that passed, he would still want to know how it had been done, fill in those gaps that still remained. He'd want to know where Hathall had met her. In the street, in a pub, as Howard had once suggested? Or had she originally been a friend of Angela's from those early London days before Hathall had been introduced to his second wife at that Finchley party? Surely she must have lived in the vicinity of Toxborough or Myringham if hers had been the job of making withdrawals from those accounts. Or had that task been shared between her and Angela? Hathall had worked only part-time at Kidd's. On his days off, Angela might have used the car to collect.

Then there was the book on Celtic languages, another strange 'exhibit' in the case he hadn't even begun to account for. Celtic languages had some, not remote, connection with archaeology, but Angela had shown no interest in them while working at the library of the National Archaeologists' League. If the book wasn't relevant, why had Hathall been so upset by the sight of it in his, Wexford's, hands?

But whatever he might deduce from the repeated examination of these facts, from carefully listing apparently unconnected pieces of information and trying to establish a link, the really important thing, the securing of Hathall before he left the country, depended now on finding evidence of that fraud. Putting those puzzle pieces together and making a picture of his chimera could wait until it was too late and Hathall was gone. That, he thought bitterly, would make an occupation for the long evenings of the New Year. And when he had still heard nothing from Lovat by Wednesday morning, he drove to Myringham to catch him in his own office, getting there by ten o'clock. Mr Lovat, he was told, was in court and wasn't expected back before lunch.

Wexford pushed his way through the crowds in Myringham's shopping precinct, climbing concrete steps, ascending and descending escalators – the whole lot strung with twinkling fairy lights in the shape of yellow and red daisies – and made his way into the magistrates' court. The public gallery was almost empty. He slid into a seat, looked round for Lovat, and spotted him sitting at the front almost under the Bench.

A pale-faced gangling man of about thirty was in the dock – according to the solicitor appearing for him, one Richard George Grey, of no fixed abode.

Ah, the husband of Morag. No wonder Lovat looked so anxious. But it didn't take long for Wexford to gather that the shop-breaking charge against Grey was based on very fragile evidence. The police, obviously, wanted a committal which it didn't look as if they would get. Grey's solicitor, youthful, suave and polished, was doing his best for his client, an effort that made Lovat's mouth turn down. With rare *schadenfreude*, Wexford found himself hoping Grey would get off. Why should he be the lucky one, able to hold a man until he had got enough evidence against him to charge him with the murder of his wife?

'And so you will appreciate, Your Worships, that my client has suffered from a series of grave misfortunes. Although he is not obliged to divulge to you any previous convictions, he wishes to do so, aware, no doubt, of how trivial you will find his one sole conviction to be. And of what does this single conviction consist? That, Your Worships, of being placed on probation for being found on enclosed premises at the tender age of seventeen.

Wexford shifted along to allow for the entry of two elderly women with shopping bags. Their expressions were avid and they seemed to make themselves at home. This entertainment, he thought, was free, matutinal, and the real nitty-gritty stuff of life, three advantages it had over the cinema. Savouring Lovat's discomfiture, he listened as the solicitor went on.

'Apart from this, what do his *criminal proclivities* amount to? Oh, it is true that when he found himself destitute and without a roof over his head, he was driven to take refuge in a derelict house for which its rightful owner had no use and which was classified as *unfit for human habitation*. But this, as Your Worships are aware, is no crime. It is not even, as the law has stood for six hundred years, trespass. It is true too that he was dismissed by his previous employer for – he frankly admits, though no charge was brought – appropriating from this employer the negligible sum of two pounds fifty. As a result, he was obliged to leave his flat or tied cottage in Maynnot Hall, Toxborough, and as an even more serious result was deserted by his wife on the ground that she refused to live with a man whose honesty was not beyond reproach. This lady, whose whereabouts are not known and whose desertion has caused my client intense distress, seems to have something in common with the Myringham police, in particular that of hitting a man when he is down ...'

There was a good deal more in the same vein. Wexford would have found it less boring, he thought, if he had heard more of the concrete evidence and less of this airy-fairy-pleading. But the evidence must have been thin and the identification of Grey shaky, for the magistrates returned after three minutes to dismiss the case. Lovat got up in disgust and Wexford rose to follow him. His elderly neighbours moved their shopping bags under protest, there was a press of people outside the court – a crowd of witnesses appearing for a grievous bodily harm case – and by the time he got through, Lovat was off in his car and not in the direction of the police station.

Well, he was fifteen miles north of Kingsmarkham, fifteen miles nearer London. Why waste those miles? Why not go on northwards for a last word with Eileen Hathall? Things could hardly be worse than they were. There was room only for improvement. And how would he feel if she were to tell him Hathall's emigration had been postponed, that he was staying a week, a fortnight, longer in London?

As he passed through Toxborough, the road taking him along Maynnot Way, a memory twitched at the back of his mind. Richard and Morag Grey had lived here once, had been servants presumably at Maynnot Hall – but it wasn't that. Yet it had something to do with what the young solicitor had said. Concentratedly, he reviewed the case, what he had come to think of as Hathall country, a landscape with figures. So many places and so many figures ... Of all the personalities he had encountered or heard spoken of, one had been hinted at by that solicitor in his dramatic address to the Bench. But no name had been mentioned except Grey's ... Yes, his wife. The lost woman, that was it. 'Deserted by his wife on the ground that she refused to live with a man whose honesty was not beyond reproach.' But what did it remind him of? Way back in Hathall country, a year ago perhaps, or months or weeks, someone somewhere had spoken to him of a woman with a peculiar regard for honesty. The trouble was that he hadn't the slightest recollection of who that someone had been.

No effort of memory was required to identify Eileen Hathall's lunch guest. Wexford hadn't seen old

Mrs Hathall for fifteen months and he was somewhat aghast to find her there. The ex-wife wouldn't tell the ex-husband of his call, but the mother would very likely tell the son. Never mind. It no longer mattered. Hathall was leaving the country in five days' time. A man who is fleeing his native land for ever has no time for petty revenges and needless precautions.

And it seemed that Mrs Hathall, who was sitting at the table drinking an after-lunch cup of tea, was under a lucky misapprehension as to the cause of his visit. This tiresome policeman had called at a house where she was before; he was calling at a house where she was again. On each previous occasion he had wanted her son, therefore – 'You won't find him here,' she said in that gruff voice with its North Country undercurrent. 'He's busy getting himself ready for going abroad.'

Eileen met his questioning glance. 'He came here last night and said good-bye,' she said. Her voice sounded calm, almost complacent. And looking from one woman to the other, Wexford realized what had happened to them. Hathall, while living in England, had been to each of them a source of chronic bitterness, breeding in the mother a perpetual need to nag and harass, in the ex-wife resentment and humiliation. Hathall gone, Hathall so far away that he might as well be dead, would leave them at peace. Eileen would take on the status almost of a widow, and the old woman would have a ready-made respectable reason – her grand-daughter's English education – as to why her son and daughter-in-law were parted.

'He's going on Monday?' he said.

Old Mrs Hathall nodded with a certain smugness. 'Don't suppose we shall ever set eyes on him again.' She finished her tea, got up and began to clear the table. The minute you finished a meal you cleared the remains of it away. That was the rule. Wexford saw her lift the lid from the teapot and contemplate its contents with an air of irritation as if she regretted the wicked waste of throwing away half a pint of tea. And she indicated to Eileen with a little dumb show that there was more if she wanted it. Eileen shook her head and Mrs Hathall bore the pot away. That Wexford might have drunk it, might at least have been given the chance to refuse it, didn't seem to cross their minds. Eileen waited till her mother-in-law had left the room.

'I'm well rid of him,' she said. 'He'd no call to come here, I'm sure. I'd done without him for five years and I can do without him for the rest of my life. As far as I'm concerned, it's good riddance.'

It was as he had supposed. She was now able to pretend to herself that she had sent him away, that now Angela was gone she could have accompanied him to Brazil herself had she so chosen. 'Mum and me,' she said, surveying the bare room, unadorned by a single bunch of holly or paper streamer, 'Mum and me'll have a quiet Christmas by ourselves. Rosemary's going to her French pen-friend tomorrow and she won't be back till her school term starts. We'll be nice and quiet on our own.'

He almost shivered. The affinity between these women frightened him. Had Eileen married Hathall because he could bring her the mother she wanted? Had Mrs Hathall chosen Eileen for him because this was the daughter she needed?

'Mum's thinking of coming to live here with me,' she said as the old woman came plodding back. 'When Rosemary goes off to college, that is. No point in keeping up two homes, is there?'

A warmer, a more affectionate, woman might have reacted by smiling her gratification or by linking an arm with this ideal daughter-in-law. Mrs Hathall's small cold eyes flickered their approval over the barren room, resting briefly on Eileen's puffy face and crimped hair, while her mouth, rigid and downturned, showed something like disappointment that she had no fault to find. 'Come along then, Eileen,' she said. 'We've got them dishes to do.'

They left Wexford to find his own way out. As he came from under the canopy that reminded him of a provincial railway station, the car that had been Hathall's turned into the drive, Rosemary at the wheel. The face that was an intelligent version of her grandmother's registered recognition but no polite expression of greeting, no smile.

'I hear you're going to France for Christmas?'

She switched off the engine but otherwise she didn't move.

'I remember you saying once before that you'd never been out of England.'

'That's right.'

'Not even on a day trip to France with your school, Miss Hathall?'

'Oh, that,' she said with icy calm. 'That was the day Angela got herself strangled.' She made a quick chilling gesture of running one finger across her throat. 'I told my mother I was going with school. I didn't. I went out with a boy instead. Satisfied?'

'Not quite. You can drive, you've been able to drive for eighteen months. You disliked Angela and seem fond of your father ...'

She interrupted him harshly. 'Fond of *him*? I can't stand the sight of any of them. My mother's a vegetable and the old woman's a cow. You don't know – no one knows – what they put me through, pulling me this way and that between them.' The words were heated but her voice didn't rise. 'I'm going to get away this year and none of them'll ever see me again for dust. Those two can live here together and one day they'll just die and no one'll find them for months.' Her hand went up to push a lock of coarse dark hair from her face, and he saw her fingertip, rosy red and quite smooth. 'Satisfied?' she said again.

'I am now.'

'Me kill Angela?' She gave a throaty laugh. 'There's others I'd kill first, I can tell you. Did you really think I'd killed her?'

'Not really,' said Wexford, 'but I'm sure you could have if you'd wanted to.'

He was rather pleased with this parting shot and thought of a few more *esprits d'escalier* as he drove off. It had only once before been his lot to confound a Hathall. He might, of course, have asked her if she had ever known a woman with a scarred fingertip, but it went against the grain with him to ask a daughter to betray her father, even such a daughter and such a father. He wasn't a medieval inquisitor or the pillar of a Fascist state.

Back at the police station he phoned Lovat who, naturally, was out and not expected to reappear till the following day. Howard wouldn't phone. If he had watched last night he had watched in vain, for Hathall had been making his farewells at Croydon.

Dora was icing the Christmas cake, placing in the centre of the white frosted circle a painted plaster Santa Claus and surrounding it with plaster robins, ornaments which came out each year from their silver paper wrappings and which had first been bought when Wexford's elder daughter was a baby.

'There! Doesn't it look nice?'

'Lovely,' said Wexford gloomily.

Dora said with calculated callousness, 'I shall be glad when that man's gone to wherever he's going and you're your normal self again.' She covered the cake and rinsed her hands. 'By the way, d'you remember once asking me about a woman called Lake? The one you said reminded you of George the Second?'

'I didn't say that,' said Wexford uneasily.

'Something like that. Well, I thought you might be interested to know she's getting married. To a man called Somerset. His wife died a couple of months ago. I imagine something has been going on there for years, but they kept it very dark. Quite a mystery.

He can't have made any death-bed promises about only taking mistresses, can he? Oh, darling, I do wish you'd show a bit of interest sometimes and not look so perpetually fed up!'

19

Thursday was his day off. Not that he would take a day off as he meant to run Lovat to earth – a fine metaphor, he thought, to use in connection with a protector of wildlife – but there was no reason for early rising. He had gone to sleep thinking what an old fool he was to suppose Nancy Lake fancied him when she was going to marry Somerset, and when morning came he was deep in a Hathall dream. This time it was totally nonsensical with Hathall and his woman embarking on to a flying 28 bus, and the phone ringing by his bed jerked him out of it at eight o'clock.

'I thought I'd get you before I left for work,' said Howard's voice. 'I've found the bus stop, Reg.'

That was more alerting than the alarm bell of the phone. 'Tell,' he said.

'I saw him leave Marcus Flower at five-thirty, and when he went up to Bond Street station I knew he'd be going to her. I had to go back to my own manor for a couple of hours, but I got down to the New King's Road by half past ten. God, it was easy. The whole exercise worked out better than I dared hope.

'I was sitting on one of the front seats downstairs, the nearside by the window. He wasn't at the stop at the top of Church Street or the next one just after Notting Hill Gate station. I knew if he was going to get on it would have to be soon and then, lo and behold, there he was all on his own at a request stop half-way up Pembridge Road. He went upstairs. I stayed on the bus and saw him get off at West End Green, and then,' Howard ended triumphantly, 'I went on to Golders Green and came home in a cab.'

'Howard, you are my only ally.'

'Well, you know what Chesterton said about that. I'll be at that bus stop from five-thirty onwards tonight and then we'll see.'

Wexford put on his dressing gown and went downstairs to find what Chesterton had said. 'There are no words to express the abyss between isolation and having one ally. It may be conceded to the mathematicians that four is twice two. But two is not twice one; two is two thousand times one ...' He felt considerably cheered. Maybe he had no force of men at his disposal but he had Howard, the resolute, the infinitely reliable, the invincible, and together they were two thousand. Two thousand and one with Lovat. He must bath and dress and get over to Myringham right away.

The head of Myringham CID was in, and with him Sergeant Hutton.

'Not a bad day,' said Lovat, peering through his funny little spectacles at the uniformly white, dull, sun-free sky.

Wexford thought it best to say nothing about Richard Grey. 'Did you get to work on that pay-roll thing?'

Lovat nodded very slowly and profoundly, but it was the sergeant who was appointed spokesman. 'We found one or two accounts which looked suspicious, sir. Three, to be precise. One was in the Trustee Savings Bank at Toxborough, one at Passingham St John and one here. All had had regular payments made into them by Kidd and Co., and in all cases the payments and withdrawals ceased in March or April of last year. The one in Myringham was in the name of a woman whose address turned out to be a sort of boarding house-cum-hotel. The people there don't remember her and we haven't been able to trace her. The one at Passingham turned out to be valid, all above board. The woman there worked at Kidd's, left in the March and just didn't bother to take the last thirty pee out of her account.'

'And the Toxborough account?'

'That's the difficulty, sir. It's in the name of a Mrs Mary Lewis and the address is a Toxborough address, but the house is shut up and the people evidently away. The neighbours say they're called Kingsbury not Lewis, but they've taken in lodgers over the years and one of them could have been a Lewis. We just have to wait till the Kingsburys come back.'

'Do these neighbours know when they're coming back?'

'No,' said Lovat.

Does anyone ever go away the week before Christmas and not stay away till after Christmas? Wexford thought it unlikely. His day off stretched before him emptily. A year ago he had resolved to be patient, but the time had come when he was counting the hours rather than the days to Hathall's departure. Four days. Ninety-six hours. And that, he thought, must be the only instance when a large number sounds pitifully smaller than a small number. Ninety-six hours. Five thousand, seven hundred and sixty minutes. Nothing. It would be gone in the twinkling of an eye ...

And the frustrating thing was that he had to waste those hours, those thousands of minutes, for there was nothing left for him personally to do. He could only go home and help Dora hang up more paper chains, arrange more coy bunches of mistletoe, plant the Christmas tree in its tub, speculate with her as to whether the turkey was small enough to lie on an oven shelf or big enough instead to be suspended by strings from the oven roof. And on Friday when only seventy-two hours remained (four thousand three hundred and twenty minutes) he went with Burden up to the police station canteen for the special

Christmas dinner. He even put on a paper hat and pulled a cracker with Policewoman Polly Davis.

Ahead of him was his tea date with Nancy Lake. He nearly phoned her to cancel it, but he didn't do this, telling himself there were still one or two questions she could answer for him and that this was as good a way as any of using up some of those four thousand-odd minutes. By four o'clock he was in Wool Lane, not thinking about her at all, thinking how, eight months before, he had walked there with Howard, full of hope and energy and determination.

'We've been lovers for nineteen years,' she said. 'I'd been married for five and I'd come to live here with my husband, and one day when I was walking in the lane I met Mark. He was in his father's garden, picking plums. We knew its proper name, but we called it a miracle tree because it was a miracle for us.'

'The jam', said Wexford, 'is very good.'

'Have some more.' She smiled at him across the table. The room where they were sitting was as bare as Eileen Hathall's and there were no Christmas decorations. But it wasn't barren or sterile or cold. He could see signs everywhere of the removal of a picture, a mirror, an ornament, and looking at her, listening to her, he could imagine the beauty and the character of those furnishings that were packed now, ready to be taken to her new home. The dark blue velvet curtains still hung at the French window, and she had drawn them to shut out the early mid-winter dusk. They made for her a sombre night sky background, and she glowed against them, her face a little flushed, the old diamond on her finger and the new diamond beside it, sparking rainbow fire from the light of the lamp at her side. 'Do you know,' she said suddenly, 'what it's like to be in love and have nowhere to go to make love?'

'I know it – vicariously.'

'We managed as best we could. My husband found out and then Mark couldn't come to Wool Lane any more. We'd tried not seeing each other and sometimes we kept it up for months, but it never worked.'

'Why didn't you marry? Neither of you had children.'

She took his empty cup and re-filled it. As she passed it to him, her fingers just brushed his and he felt himself grow hot with something that was almost anger. As if it wasn't bad enough, he thought, her being there and looking like that without all this sex talk as well. 'My husband died,' she said. 'We were going to marry. Then Mark's wife got ill and he couldn't leave her. It was impossible.'

He couldn't keep the sneering note out of his voice. 'So you remained faithful to each other and lived in hopes?'

'No, there were others – for me.' She looked at him steadily, and he found himself unable to return that look. 'Mark knew, and if he minded he never blamed me. How could he? I told you once, I felt like a distraction, something to – to divert him when he could be spared from his wife's bedside.'

'Was it she you meant when you asked me if it was wrong to wish for someone's death?'

'Of course. Who else? Did you think – did you think I was speaking of *Angela*?' Her gravity went and she was smiling again. 'Oh, my dear ...! Shall I tell you something else? Two years ago when I was very bored and very lonely because Gwen Somerset was home from hospital and wouldn't let Mark out of her sight, I – I made advances to Robert Hathall. There's a confession for you! And he wouldn't have me. He turned me down. I am not accustomed,' she said with mock pomposity, 'to being turned down.'

'I suppose not. Do you think I'm blind,' he said rather savagely, 'or a complete fool?'

'Just unapproachable. If you've finished, shall we go into the other room? It's more comfortable. I haven't yet stripped it of every vestige of me.'

His questions were answered, and there was no need now to ask where she had been when Angela died or where Somerset had been, or probe any of those mysteries about her and Somerset, which were mysteries no more. He might as well say good-bye and go, he thought, as he crossed the hall behind her and followed her into a warmer room of soft textures and deep rich colours, and where there seemed no hard surfaces, but only silk melting into velvet and velvet into brocade. Before she could close the door, he held out his hand to her, meaning to begin a little speech of thanks and farewell. But she took his hand in both of hers.

'I shall be gone on Monday,' she said, looking up into his face. 'The new people are moving in. We

218

shan't meet again. I would promise you that, if you like.'

Up till then he had doubted her intentions towards him. There was no room for doubt now.

'Why should you think I want to be the last fling for a woman who is going to her first love?'

'Isn't it a compliment?'

He said, 'I'm an old man, and an old man who is taken in by compliments is pathetic.'

She flushed a little. 'I shall soon be an old woman. We could be pathetic together.' A rueful laugh shook her voice. 'Don't go yet. We can – talk. We've never really talked yet.'

'We have done nothing but talk,' said Wexford, but he didn't go. He let her lead him to the sofa and sit beside him and talk to him about Somerset and Somerset's wife and the nineteen years of secrecy and deception. Her hand rested in his, and as he relaxed and listened to her, he remembered the first time he had held it and what she had said when he had kept hold of it a fraction too long. At last she got up. He also rose and put that hand to his lips. 'I wish you happy,' he said. 'I hope you're going to be very happy.'

'I'm a little afraid, you know, of how it will be after so long. Do you understand what I mean?'

'Of course.' he spoke gently, all savagery gone, and when she asked him to have a drink with her, he said, 'I'll drink *to* you and to your happiness.'

She put her arms round his neck and kissed him. The kiss was impulsive, light, over before he could respond to her or resist her. She was gone from the room for some minutes, more minutes than were needful to fetch drinks and glasses. He heard the sound of her footsteps overhead, and he guessed how she would be when she came back. So he had to decide what he should do, whether to go or stay. Gather ye rosebuds, roses, other men's flowers, while ye may? Or be an old man, dreaming dreams and being mindful of one's marriage vows?

The whole of his recent life seemed to him a long series of failures, of cowardice and caution. And yet the whole of his recent life had also been bent towards doing what he believed to be right and just. Perhaps, in the end, it came to the same thing.

At last he went out into the hall. He called her name, 'Nancy!', using that name for the first and only time, and when he moved to the foot of the stairs, he saw her at the head of them. The light there was soft and kind, unnecessarily kind, and she was as he had known she would be, as he had seen her in his fantasies – only better than that, better than his expectations.

He looked up at her in wondering appreciation, looked for long silent minutes. But by then he had made up his mind.

Only the unwise dwell on what is past with regret for rejected opportunity or nostalgia for chosen delight. He regretted nothing, for he had only done what any man of sense would have done in his position. His decision had been reached during those moments while she had been away from the room and he had stuck to that decision, confident he was acting according to his own standards and what was right for him. But he was astonished to find it was so late when he let himself into his own house, nearly eight o'clock. And at the recalling of his mind to time's passing, he was back to counting the minutes, back to calculating that only about three and a half thousand of them remained. Nancy's face faded, the warmth of her vanished. He marched into the kitchen where Dora was making yet another batch of mince pies and said rather brusquely, 'Has Howard phoned?'

She looked up. He had forgotten – he was always forgetting – how astute she was. 'He wouldn't phone at this time, would he? It's last thing at night or first thing in the morning with him.'

'Yes, I know. But I'm strung up about this thing.'

'Indeed you are. You forgot to kiss me.'

So he kissed her, and the immediate past was switched off. No regrets, he reminded himself, no nostalgia, no introspection. And he took a mince pie and bit into the hot crisp crust.

'You'll get fat and gross and revolting.'

'Perhaps,' said Wexford thoughtfully, 'that wouldn't be such a bad thing – in moderation, of course.'

20

Sheila Wexford, the chief inspector's actress daughter, arrived on Saturday morning. It was good to see her in the flesh, her father said, instead of two-dimensionally and monotonally in her television serial. She pranced about the house, arranging the cards more artistically and singing that she was dreaming of a white Christmas. It seemed, however, that it was going to be a foggy one. The long-range weather forecast had said it would be, and now the weather signs themselves fulfilled this prediction as a white morning mist shrouded the sun at noon and by evening was dense and yellowish.

The shortest day of the year. The Winter Solstice. It was arctic in light as well as in temperature, the fog closing out daylight at three and heralding seventeen hours of darkness. Along the streets lighted Christmas trees showed only as an amber blur in windows. God rest you merry, gentlemen, let nothing you dismay ... Seventeen hours of darkness, thirty-six hours to go.

Howard had promised to phone and did so at ten. Hathall had been indoors alone at 62 Dartmeet Avenue since three. Howard was in the call-box opposite the house, but now he was going home. His six watching nights to Christmas were over – today's had been a bonus vigil, undertaken because he couldn't bear to be beaten and he was going home.

'I'll watch him tomorrow, Reg, for the last time.'

'Is there any point?'

'I shall feel I've done the job as thoroughly as it can be done.'

Hathall had been alone most of the day. Did that mean he had sent the woman on ahead of him? Wexford went to bed early and lay awake thinking of Christmas, thinking of himself and Howard retired to a quiet corner and holding their last inquest over what had happened, what else they could have done, what might have happened if on 2 October a year ago Griswold hadn't issued his ban.

On Sunday morning the fog began to lift. The vague hope Wexford had entertained that fog might force Hathall to postpone his departure faded as the sun appeared strong and bright by midday. He listened to the radio news but no airports were closed and no flights cancelled. And as the evening began with a bright sunset and a clear frosty sky

– as if winter was already dying with the passing of the solstice – he knew he must resign himself to Hathall's escape. It was all over.

But though he could teach himself to avoid introspection where Nancy Lake was concerned, he couldn't help dwelling with regret and bitterness over the long period during which he and Robert Hathall had been adversaries. Things might have been very different if only he had guessed at that payroll fraud – if fraud there was – before. He should have known too that an angry paranoiac with much at stake wouldn't react passively to his clumsy probing and what that probing implied. But it was all over now and he would never know who the woman was. Sadly he thought of other questions that must remain unanswered. What was the reason for the presence in Bury Cottage of the Celtic languages book? Why had Hathall, who in middle life had come to enjoy sexual variety, repulsed such a woman as Nancy Lake? Why had his accomplice, in most ways so thorough and careful, left her handprint on, of all places, the side of the bath? And why had Angela, anxious to please her mother-in-law, desperate for a reconciliation, worn on the day of her visit the very clothes which had helped turn her mother-in-law against her?

It didn't cross his mind that, at this late stage, Howard would have any further success. Hathall's habit was to stay at home on Sundays, entertaining his mother or his daughter. And even though he had already said good-bye to them, there seemed no reason to suppose he would change his ways to the extent of going to Notting Hill and her, when they were leaving together on the following day. So when he lifted the receiver at eleven that Sunday night and heard the familiar voice, a little tired now and a little irritable, he thought at first Howard was phoning only to say at what time he and Denise would arrive on Christmas Eve. And when he understood the true reason for the call, that at last when it was too late, Howard was on the brink of accomplishing his task, he felt the sick despair of a man who doesn't want hope to come in and threaten his resignation.

'You saw her?' he said dully. 'You actually saw her?'

'I know how you're feeling, Reg, but I have to tell you. I couldn't keep it to myself. I saw him. I saw her. I saw them together. And I lost them.'

'Oh, *God*. My God, it's more than I can take.'

'Don't kill the messenger, Reg,' Howard said gently. 'Don't do a Cleopatra on me. I that do bring the news made not the match.'

'I'm not angry with you. How could I be after all you've done? I'm angry with – fate, I suppose. Tell me what happened.'

'I started watching the house in Dartmeet Avenue after lunch. I didn't know whether Hathall was in or not until I saw him come out and put a great sackful of rubbish into one of those dustbins. He was having a clear-out, packing, I expect, and throwing out what he didn't want. I sat there in the car, and I nearly went home when I saw his light go on at half past four.

'Maybe it would have been better if I had gone home. At least I couldn't have raised your hopes. He came out of the house at six, Reg, and walked down to West End Green. I followed him in the car and parked in Mill Lane – that's the street that runs westwards off Fortune Green Road. We both waited for about five minutes. The 28 bus didn't come and he got into a taxi instead.'

'You followed it?' said Wexford, admiration for a moment overcoming his bitterness.

'It's easier to follow a taxi than a bus. Buses keep stopping. 'Following a taxi in London on a Sunday night is a different matter from trying to do it by day in the rush hours. Anyway, the driver took more or less the same route as the bus. It dropped Hathall outside a pub in Pembridge Road.'

'Near that stop where you saw him get on the bus before?'

'Quite near, yes. I've been to that bus stop and the streets round about it every night this week, Reg. But he must have used the back street to get to her from Notting Hill Gate station. I never saw him once.'

'You went into this pub after him?'

'It's called the Rosy Cross and it was very crowded. He bought two drinks, gin for himself and pernod for her, although she hadn't come in yet. He managed to find two seats in a corner and he put his coat on one of them to keep it. Most of the time the crowd blocked my view of him, but I could see that glass of yellow pernod waiting on the table for her to come and drink it.

'Hathall was early or she was ten minutes late. I didn't know she'd come in till I saw a hand go round that yellow glass and the glass lifted up out of my sight. I moved then and pushed through the crowd to get a better look. It was the same woman I saw him with outside Marcus Flower, a pretty woman in her early thirties with dyed blonde cropped hair. No, don't ask. I didn't see her hand. I was too close for safety as it was. I think Hathall recognized me. God, he'd have to be blind not to by now, even with the care I've taken.

'They drank their drinks quite quickly and pushed their way out. She must live quite near there, but where she lives I can't tell you. It doesn't matter now, anyway. I saw them walking away when I came out and I was going to follow them on foot. A taxi came and they got into it. Hathall didn't even wait to tell the driver where he wanted to go. He just got in and must have given his instructions afterwards. He wasn't going to run the risk of being followed, and I couldn't follow them. The taxi went off up Pembridge Road and I lost them. I lost them and went home.

'The last of Robert Hathall, Reg. It was good while it lasted. I really thought – well, never mind. You were right all along the line and that, I'm afraid, must be your consolation.'

Wexford said good night to his nephew and that he would see him on Christmas Eve. An aircraft sounded overhead, coming out of Gatwick. He stood by his bedroom window and watched its white and red lights like meteors crossing the clear

227

starlit sky. Just a few more hours and Hathall would be on such an aircraft. First thing in the morning? Or an afternoon flight? Or would he and she be going by night? He found he knew very little about extradition. It hadn't come in his way to know about it. And things had taken such strange turns lately that a country would probably bargain, would want concessions or some sort of exchange before releasing a foreign national. Besides, though you might get an extradition order if you had irrefutable evidence of murder, surely you wouldn't on a fraud charge. Deception, the charge would be, he thought, deception under Section 15 of the Theft Act of 1968. It suddenly seemed fantastic to contemplate putting all that political machinery in motion to fetch a man out of Brazil for helping himself to the funds of a plastic doll factory.

He thought of Crippen being apprehended in mid-Atlantic by a wireless message, of train robbers caught after long periods of freedom in the distant South, of films he had seen in which some criminal, at ease now and believing himself secure, felt the heavy hand of the law descend on his shoulder as he sat drinking wine in a sunny pavement café. It wasn't his world. He couldn't see himself, even in a minor capacity, taking part in exotic drama. Instead he saw Hathall flying away to freedom, to the life he had planned and had done murder to get, while in a week or two perhaps Brock Lovat was obliged to admit defeat because he had found no fraud or theft or deception but only a few vague hints of something underhand which Hathall might have been called to account for – if only Hathall had been there to answer.

The day had come.

Waking early, Wexford thought of Hathall waking early too. He had seen Howard the night before, had suspected he was still being followed, so wouldn't have dared spend the night with the woman or have her spend the night with him. Now he was washing at the sink in that nasty little room, taking a suit from the Battle of Mons wardrobe, shaving before packing his razor into the small hand-case he would take with him in the aircraft. Wexford could see the red granite face, more heavily flushed from its contact with the razor's edge, the thinning black hair slicked back with a wet comb. Now Hathall would be taking a last look at the ten by twelve cell which had been his home for nine months, and thinking with happy anticipation of the home that was to be his; now across to the call-box, at mid-winter daybreak, to check his flight with the airport and harangue the girl who spoke to him for not being prompt enough or efficient or considerate enough; now, lastly, a call to *her*, wherever she was, in the labyrinth of Notting Hill. No, perhaps one more call. To the taxi rank or car-hire place for the car that would take him and his luggage away for ever ...

Stop it, he told himself severely. Leave it. No more of this. This way madness – or at least an obsessional neurosis – lies. Christmas is coming, go to work, forget him. He took Dora a cup of tea and went to work.

In his office he went through the morning mail and stuck a few Christmas cards around. There was one from Nancy Lake, which he looked at thoughtfully for a moment or two before putting it inside his desk. No less than five calendars had come, including one of the glossy nudes *genre*, the offering of a local garage. It brought to mind Ginge at West Hampstead station, the offices of Marcus Flower ... Was he going crazy? What was happening to him when he let erotica bring to mind a murder hunt? Stop it. From his selection he chose a handsome and immensely dull calendar, twelve colour plates of Sussex scenes, and pinned it on to the wall next to the district map. The gift of a grateful garage he put into a new envelope, marked it *For Your Eyes Only* and had it sent down to Burden's office. That would set the prim inspector fulminating against current moral standards and divert his, Wexford's, mind from that bloody, unspeakable, triumphant, Goddamned crook and fugitive, Robert Hathall.

Then he turned his attention to the matters that were at present concerning Kingsmarkham police. Five women in the town and two from outlying villages had complained of obscene telephone calls. The only extraordinary thing about that was that their caller had also been a woman. Wexford smiled a little to note the odd corners of life into which Women's Liberation was infiltrating. He smiled more grimly and with exasperation at Sergeant Martin's attempt to make an issue out of the activities of four small boys who had tied a length of string from a lamp-post to a garden wall in an effort to trip up passers-by. Why did they waste his time with this rubbish? Yet sometimes it is better to have one's time wasted than spent on hankering ever and ever after a vain thing ...

His internal phone was bleeping. He lifted the receiver, expecting the voice of a self-righteous and indignant Burden.

'Chief Inspector Lovat to see you, sir. Shall I show him up?'

21

Lovat came in slowly, and with him his inevitable interpreter, his *fidus Achates*, Sergeant Hutton.

'Lovely day.'

'Be damned to the day,' said Wexford in a throaty voice because his heart and his blood pressure were behaving very strangely. 'Never mind the day. I wish it would bloody well snow, I wish ...'

Hutton said quietly, 'If we might just sit down a while, sir? Mr Lovat has something to tell you which he thinks will interest you greatly. And since it was you put him on to it, it seemed only a matter of courtesy ...'

'Sit down, do as you like, have a calendar, take one each. I know why you've come. But just tell me one thing. Can you get a man extradited for what you've found out? Because if you can't, you've had it. Hathall's going to Brazil today, and ten to one he's gone already.'

'Dear me,' said Lovat placidly.

Wexford nearly put his head in his hands. 'Well, can you?' he shouted.

'I'd better tell you what Mr Lovat *has* found, sir. We called at the home of Mr and Mrs Kingsbury again last night. They'd just returned. They'd been on a visit to their married daughter who was having a baby. No Mrs Mary Lewis has never lodged with them and they have never had any connection with Kidd and Co. Moreover, on making further enquiries at the boarding house Mr Lovat told you about, he could discover no evidence at all of the existence of the other so-called account holder.'

'So you've had a warrant sworn for Hathall's arrest?'

'Mr Lovat would like to talk to Robert Hathall, sir,' said Hutton cautiously. 'I'm sure you'll agree we need a little more to go on. Apart from the – er, courtesy of the matter, we called on you for Hathall's present address.'

'His present address,' Wexford snapped, 'is probably about five miles up in the air above Maderia or wherever that damned plane flies.'

'Unfortunate,' said Lovat, shaking his head.

'Maybe he hasn't left, sir. If we could phone him?'

'I daresay you could if he had a phone and if he hasn't left.' Wexford looked in some despair at the clock. It was ten-thirty. 'Frankly, I don't know what to do. The only thing I can suggest is that we all get out to Millerton-*les-deux* – er, Hightrees Farm, and lay all this before the chief constable.'

'Good idea,' said Lovat. 'Many a fine night I've spent watching the badger setts there.'

Wexford could have kicked him.

He never knew what prompted him to ask the question. There was no sixth sense about it. Perhaps it was just that he thought he should have the facts of this fraud as straight in his mind as they were in Hutton's. But he did ask it, and afterwards he thanked God he had asked it then on the country lane drive to Millerton.

'The addresses of the account holders, sir? One was in the name of Mrs Dorothy Carter of Ascot House, Myringham – that's the boarding house place – and the other of Mrs Mary Lewis at 19 Maynnot Way, Toxborough.'

'Did you say Maynnot Way?' Wexford asked in a voice that sounded far away and unlike his own.

'That's right. It runs from the industrial estate to ...'

'I know where it runs to, sergeant. I also know who lived at Maynnot Hall in the middle of Maynnot Way.' He felt a constriction in his throat. 'Brock,' he said, 'what were you doing at Kidd's that day I met you at the gates?'

Lovat looked at Hutton and Hutton said, 'Mr Lovat was pursuing his enquiries in connection with the disappearance of Morag Grey, sir. Morag Grey worked as a cleaner at Kidd's for a short while when her husband was gardener at the hall. Naturally, we explored every way open to us.'

'You haven't explored Maynnot Way enough.' Wexford almost gasped at the enormity of his discovery. His chimera, he thought, his thing of fanciful conception. 'Your Morag Grey isn't buried in anyone's garden. She's Robert Hathall's woman, she's going off to Brazil with him. My God, I can see it all ...!' If only he had Howard beside him to explain all this to instead of the phlegmatic Lovat and this open-mouthed sergeant. 'Listen,' he said. 'This Grey woman was Hathall's accomplice in the fraud. He met her when they both worked at Kidd's, and she and his wife had the job of making withdrawals from those accounts. No doubt, she thought up the name and address of Mrs Mary Lewis because she knew Maynnot Way and knew the Kingsburys let rooms. Hathall fell for her and she murdered Hathall's wife. She isn't dead, Brock, she's been living in London as Hathall's mistress ever since ... When did she disappear?'

'As far as we know, in August or September of last year, sir,' said the sergeant, and he brought the car to a halt on the gravel outside Hightrees Farm.

For the sake of the reputation of Mid-Sussex, it would be most unfortunate for Hathall to escape. This, to Wexford's amazement, was the opinion of Charles Griswold. And he saw a faint flush of unease colour the statesman-like face as the chief constable was forced to admit the theory was tenable.

'This is a little more than "feeling", I think, Reg,' he

said, and it was he personally who phoned London Airport.

Wexford and Lovat and Hutton had to wait a long time before he came back. And when he did it was to say that Robert Hathall and a woman travelling as Mrs Hathall were on the passenger list of a flight leaving for Rio de Janeiro at twelve forty-five. The airport police would be instructed to hold them both on a charge of deception under the Theft Act, and a warrant had better be sworn at once.

'She must be travelling on his passport.'

'Or on Angela's,' Wexford said. 'He's still got it. I remember looking at it, but it was left with him in Bury Cottage.'

'No need to be bitter, Reg. Better late than never.'

'It happens, sir,' said Wexford very politely but with an edge to his voice, 'to be twenty to twelve now. I just hope we're in time.'

'Oh, he won't get out now,' Griswold said on a breezy note. 'They'll stop him at the airport where you can take yourselves forthwith. Forthwith, Reg. And tomorrow morning you can come over for a Christmas drink and tell me all about it.'

They went back to Kingsmarkham to pick up Burden. The inspector was in the foyer, peering through his glasses at the envelope he brandished, and angrily enquiring of a puzzled station sergeant who had had the effrontery to send him pornography for his exclusive perusal.

'Hathall?' he said when Wexford explained. 'You don't mean it. You're joking.'

'Get in the car, Mike, and I'll tell you on the way. No, Sergeant Hutton will tell *us* on the way. What have you got there? Art studies? Now I see why you needed glasses.'

Burden gave a snort of rage and was about to launch into a long explanation of his innocence, but Wexford cut him short. He didn't need diversions now. He had been waiting for this day, this moment, for fifteen months, and he could have shouted his triumph at the crisp blue air, the spring-like sun. They left in two cars. The first contained Lovat and his driver and Polly Davis, the second Wexford, Burden and Sergeant Hutton with their driver.

'I want to know everything you can tell me about Morag Grey.'

'She was – well, is – a Scot, sir. From the north-west of Scotland, Ullapool. But there's not much work up there and she came south and went into service. She met Grey seven or eight years ago and married him and they got that job at Maynnot Hall.'

'What, he did the garden and she cleaned the place?'

'That's right. I don't quite know why as she seems to have been a cut above that sort of thing. According to her mother and – more to the point – according to her employer at the hall, she'd had a reasonable sort of education and was quite bright. Her mother says Grey had dragged her down.'

'How old is she and what does she look like?'

'She'd be about thirty-two now, sir. Thin, dark-haired, nothing special. She did some of the housework at the hall and did outside cleaning jobs as well. One of those was at Kidd's, in last March twelvemonth, but she only stayed two or three weeks. Then Grey got the sack for taking a couple of quid from his employer's wife's handbag. They had to leave their flat and go and squat in Myringham Old Town. But soon after that Morag turned him out. Grey says she found out the reason for their getting the push and wouldn't go on living with a thief. A likely story, I'm sure you'll agree, sir. But he insisted on it, despite the fact that he went straight from her to another woman who had a room about a mile away on the other side of Myringham.'

'It doesn't,' said Wexford thoughtfully, 'seem a likely story under the circumstances.'

'He says he spent the money he pinched on a present for her, a gilt snake necklace ...'

'Ah.'

'Which may be true but doesn't prove much.'

'I wouldn't say that, Sergeant. What happened to her when she was left on her own?'

'We know very little about that. Squatters don't really have neighbours, they're an itinerant population. She had a series of cleaning jobs up until August and then she went on Social Security. All we know is that Morag told a woman in that row of houses that she'd got a good job in the offing and would be moving away. What that job was and where she was going we never found out. No one saw her after the middle of September. Grey came back around Christmas and took away what possessions she'd left behind.'

'Didn't you say it was her mother who started the hue and cry?'

'Morag had been a regular correspondent, and when her mother got no answers to her letters she wrote to Grey. He found the letters when he went back at Christmas and at last he wrote back with some cock-and-bull story about thinking his wife had gone to Scotland. Mother had never trusted Richard Grey and she went to the police. She came down here and we had to get an interpreter in on account of – believe it or not – her speaking only Gaelic.'

Wexford, who at that moment felt, like the White Queen, that he could have believed six impossible things before breakfast, said, 'Does Morag also – er, have the Gaelic?'

'Yes, sir, she does. She's bilingual.'

With a sigh Wexford sank back against the upholstery. There were a few loose ends to be tied, a few small instances of the unaccountable to be accounted for, but otherwise ... He closed his eyes. The car was going very slowly. Vaguely he wondered, but without looking, if they were running into heavy traffic as they approached London. It didn't matter. Hathall would have been stopped by now, detained in some little side room of the airport. Even if he hadn't been told why he wasn't allowed to fly, he would know. He would know it was all over. The car was almost stopping. Wexford opened his eyes and seized Burden's arm. He wound down the window.

'See,' he said, pointing to the ground that now slid

past at a snail's pace. 'It does move. And that ...' his arm went upwards, skywards, '... that doesn't.'

'What doesn't?' said Burden. 'There's nothing to see. Look for yourself. We're fogbound.'

22

It was nearly four o'clock before they reached the airport. All aircraft were grounded, and Christmas holiday travellers filled the lounges while queues formed at enquiry desks. The fog was all-enveloping, fluffy like aerated snow, dense earthbound clouds of it, a white gas that set people coughing and covering their faces.

Hathall wasn't there.

The fog had begun to come down at Heathrow at eleven-thirty, but it had affected other parts of London earlier than that. Had he been among the hundreds who had phoned the airport from fogbound outer suburbs to enquire if their flights would leave? There was no way of knowing. Wexford walked slowly and painstakingly through the lounges, from bar to restaurant, out on to the observation terraces, looking into every face, tired faces, indignant faces, bored faces. Hathall wasn't there.

'According to the weather forecast,' said Burden, 'the fog'll lift by evening.'

'And according to the long-range, it's going to be a white Christmas, a white fog Christmas. You and Polly stay here, Mike. Get on to the chief constable and fix it so that we have every exit watched, not just Heathrow.'

So Burden and Polly remained while Wexford and Lovat and Hutton began the long drive to Hampstead. It was very slow going. Streams of traffic, bound for the M1, blocked all the north-west roads as the fog, made tawny by the yellow overhead lights, cast a blinding pall over the city. The landmarks on the route, which by now were all too familiar, had lost their sharp outlines and become amorphous. The winding hills of Hampstead lay under a smoky shroud and the great trees of Hampstead loomed like black clouds before being swallowed up in paler vapour. They crawled into Dartmeet Avenue at ten minutes to seven and pulled up outside number 62. The house was in darkness, every window tight shut and dead black. The dustbins were dewed where the fog had condensed on them. Their lids were scattered, and a cat darted out from under one of them, a chicken bone in its mouth. As Wexford got out of the car, the fog caught at his throat. He thought of another foggy day in Myringham Old Town, of men digging in vain for a body that had never been there. He thought of how his whole pursuit of Hathall had been befogged by doubt and confusion and obstruction, and then he went up to the front door and rang the landlord's bell.

He had rung it twice more before a light showed through the pane of glass above the lintel. At last the door was opened by the same little elderly man Wexford had once before seen come out and fetch his cat. He was smoking a thin cigar and he showed neither surprise nor interest when the chief inspector said who he was and showed him his warrant card.

'Mr Hathall left last night,' he said.

'Last night?'

'That's right. To tell you the truth, I didn't expect him to go till this morning. He'd paid his rent up to tonight. But he got hold of me in a bit of a hurry last night and said he'd decided to go, so it wasn't for me to argue, was it?'

The hall was icy cold, in spite of the oil heater which stood at the foot of the stairs, and the place reeked of burning oil and cigar smoke. Lovat rubbed his hands together, then held them out over the guttering blue and yellow flames.

'Mr Hathall came back here about eight last night in a taxi,' said the landlord. 'I was out in the front garden, calling my cat. He came up to me and said he wanted to vacate his room there and then.'

'How did he seem?' Wexford said urgently. 'Worried? Upset?'

'Nothing out of the way. He was never what you'd call a pleasant chap. Always grumbling about something. We went up to his room for me to take the inventory. I always insist on that before I give them back their deposits. D'you want to go up now? There's nothing to see, but you can if you want.'

Wexford nodded and they mounted the stairs. The hall and the landing were lit by the kind of lights that go off automatically after two minutes, and they went off now before Hathall's door was reached. In the pitch dark the landlord cursed, fumbling for his keys and for the light switch. And Wexford, his nerves tautening again, let out a grunt of shock when something snaked along the banister rail and jumped for the landlord's shoulder. It was, of course, only the cat. The light went on, the key was found, and the door opened.

The room was stuffy and musty as well as cold. Wexford saw Hutton's lip curl as he glanced at the First World War wardrobe, the fireside chairs and the ugly paintings, as he thought no doubt of an inventory being taken of this Junk City rubbish. Thin blankets lay untidily folded on the bare mattress beside a bundle of nickel knives and forks secured with a rubber band, a whistling kettle with a string-bound handle and a plaster vase that still bore on its base the price ticket indicating that it had cost thirty-five pence.

The cat ran along the mantelpiece and leapt on to the screen. 'I knew there was something fishy about him, mind you,' said the landlord.

'How? What gave you that idea?'

He favoured Wexford with a rather contemptuous smile. 'I've seen you before, for one thing. I can spot a copper a mile off. And there was always folks watching him. I don't miss much, though I don't say much either. I spotted the little fellow with the ginger hair – made me laugh when he came here and said he was from the council – and the tall thin one that was always in a car.'

'Then you'll know,' Wexford said, swallowing his humiliation, 'why he was watched.'

'Not me. He never did nothing but come and go and have his mother to tea and grouse about the rent.'

'He never had a woman come here? A woman with short fair hair?'

'Not him. His mother and his daughter, that's all. That's who he told me they were, and I reckon it was true seeing they was the spitting image of him. Come on, puss, let's get back where it's warm.'

Turning wearily away, standing on the spot where Hathall had been on the point of flinging him down those stairs, Wexford said, 'You gave him back his deposit and he left. What time was that?'

'About nine.' The landing light went off again and again the landlord flicked the switch, muttering under his breath while the cat purred on his shoulder. 'He was going abroad somewhere, he said. There were a lot of labels on his cases but I didn't look close. I like to see what they're doing, you know, keep an eye till they're off the premises. He went over the road and made a phone call and then a taxi came and took him off.'

They went down into the smelly hall. The light went off and this time the landlord didn't switch it on. He closed the door on them quickly to keep out the fog.

'He could have gone last night,' said Wexford to Lovat. 'He could have crossed to Paris or Brussels or Amsterdam and flown from there.'

'But why should he?' Hutton objected. 'Why should he think we're on to him after all this time?'

Wexford didn't want to tell them, at this stage, about Howard's involvement or Howard's encounter with Hathall on the previous evening. But it had come sharply into his mind up in that cold deserted room. Hathall had seen Howard at about seven, had recognized this man who was tailing him, and soon after had given him the slip. The taxi he had got into had dropped the girl off and taken him back to Dartmeet Avenue where he had settled with his landlord, taken his luggage and gone. Gone where? Back to her first and then ...? Wexford shrugged unhappily and went across the road to the call-box.

Burden's voice told him the airport was still fogbound. The place was swarming with disappointed stranded would-be travellers, and swarming by now with anxious police. Hathall hadn't appeared. If he had phoned, along with hundreds of other callers, he hadn't given his name.

'But he knows we're on to him,' said Burden.

'What d'you mean?'

'D'you remember a chap called Aveney? Manager of Kidd's?'

'Of course I remember. What the hell is this?'

'He got a phone call from Hathall at his home at nine last night. Hathall wanted to know – asked in a roundabout way, mind you – if we'd been asking questions about him. And Aveney, the fool, said not about his wife, that was all over, but only looking into the books in case there was something fishy about the pay-roll.'

'How do we know all this?' Wexford asked dully.

'Aveney had second thoughts, wondered if he ought to have told him anything, though he knew our enquiries had come to nothing. Apparently, he tried to get hold of you this morning and when he couldn't he at last contacted Mr Griswold.'

That, then, was the phone call Hathall had made from the call-box in Dartmeet Avenue, this very call-box, after leaving the landlord and before getting into that taxi. That, coupled with his recognition of Howard, would have been enough to frighten the wits out of him. Wexford went back across the road and got into the car where Lovat was smoking one of his nasty little damp cigarettes.

'I think the fog's thinning, sir,' said Hutton.

'Maybe. What time is it?'

'Ten to eight. What do we do now? Get back to the airport or try and find Morag Grey's place?'

With patient sarcasm, Wexford said, 'I have been trying to do that for nine months, Sergeant, the normal period of gestation, and I've brought forth nothing. Maybe you think you can do better in a couple of hours.'

'We could at least go back through Notting Hill, sir, instead of taking the quicker way by the North Circular.'

'Oh, do as you like,' Wexford snapped, and he flung himself into the corner as far as possible from Lovat and his cigarette which smelt as bad as the landlord's cigar. Badgers! Country coppers, he thought unfairly. Fools who couldn't make a simple charge like shop-breaking stick. What did Hutton think Notting Hill was? A village like Passingham St John where everyone knew everyone else and would be all agog and raring to gossip because a neighbour had gone off to foreign parts?

They followed the 28 bus route. West End Lane, Quex Road, Kilburn High Road, Kilburn Park ... The fog was decreasing, moving now, lying here in dense patches, there shivering and thinning into streaks. And Christmas colours began to glitter through it, garish paper banners in windows, sharp little starry lights that winked on and off. Shirland Road, Great Western Road, Pembridge Villas, Pembridge Road ...

One of these, Wexford thought, sitting up, must be the bus stop where Howard had seen Hathall board the 28. Streets debouched everywhere, streets that led into other streets, into squares, into a vast multitudinously peopled hinterland. Let Hutton make what he could of ...

'Stop the car, will you?' he said quickly.

Pink light streamed across the roadway from the glazed doors of a public house. Wexford had seen its sign and remembered. The Rosy Cross. If they had been regular customers, if they had often met there, the licensee or a barman might recall them. Perhaps they had met there again last night before leaving or had gone back just to say good-bye. At least he would know. This way he might know for sure.

The interior was an inferno of light and noise and smoke. The crowd was of a density and a conviviality usually only reached much later in the evening, but this was Christmas, the night before the Eve. Not only was every table occupied and every bar stool and place by the bar, but every square foot of floor space too where people stood packed, pressed against each other, their cigarettes sending spirals of smoke to mingle with the blue pall that hung between gently swaying paper chains and smarting screwed-up eyes. Wexford pushed his way to the bar. Two barmen and a girl were working it, serving drinks feverishly, wiping down the counter, slopping dirty glasses into a steaming sink.

'And the next?' called the older of the barmen, the licensee maybe. His face was red, his forehead gleaming with sweat and his grey hair plastered against it in wet curls. 'What's for you, sir?'

Wexford said, 'Police. I'm looking for a tall black-haired man, about forty-five, and a younger blonde woman.' His elbow was jostled and he felt a trickle of beer run down his wrist. 'They were in here last night. The name is …'

'They don't give their names. There were about five hundred people in here last night.'

'I've reason to think they came in here regularly.'

The barman shrugged. 'I have to attend to my customers. Can you wait ten minutes?'

But Wexford thought he had waited long enough. Let it pass into other hands, he could do no more. Struggling through the press of people, he made again for the door, bemused by the colours and the lights and the smoke and the heady reek of liquor. There seemed to be coloured shapes everywhere, the circles of red and purple balloons, the shining translucent cones of liqueur bottles, the squares of stained window glass. His head swimming, he realized he hadn't eaten all day. Red and purple circles, orange and blue paper spheres, here a green glass square, there a bright yellow rectangle ...

A bright yellow rectangle. His head cleared. He steadied and stilled himself. Jammed between a man in a leather coat and a girl in a fur coat, he looked through a tiny space that wasn't cluttered by skirts and legs and chair legs and handbags, looked through the blue acrid smoke at that yellow rectangle which was liquid in a tall glass, and saw it raised by a hand and carried out of his sight.

Pernod. Not a popular drink in England. Ginge had drunk it mixed with Guinness as a Demon King. And one other, she that he sought, his chimera, his thing of fanciful conception, drank it diluted and yellowed by water. He moved slowly, pushing his way towards that corner table where she was, but he could only get within three yards of her. There were too many people. But now there was a space clear enough at eye level for him to see her, and he looked long and long, staring greedily as a man in love stares at the woman whose coming he has awaited for months on end.

She had a pretty face, tired and wan. Her eyes were smarting from the smoke and her cropped blonde hair showed half an inch of dark at the roots. She was alone, but the chair beside her was covered by a folded coat, a man's coat, and stacked against the wall behind her, piled at her feet and walling her in, were half a dozen suitcases. She lifted her glass again and sipped from it, not looking at him at all, but darting quick nervous glances towards a heavy mahogany door marked *Telephone and Toilets*. But Wexford lingered, looking his fill at his chimera made flesh, until hats and hair and faces converged and cut off his view.

He opened the mahogany door and slipped into a passage. Two more doors faced him, and at the end of the passage was a glass kiosk. Hathall was bent over the phone inside it, his back to Wexford. Phoning the airport, Wexford thought, phoning to see if his flight's on now the fog is lifting. He stepped into the men's lavatory, pulling the door to, waiting till he heard Hathall's footsteps pass along the passage.

The mahogany door swung and clicked shut. Wexford let a minute go by and then he too went back into the bar. The cases were gone, the yellow glass empty. Thrusting people aside, ignoring expostulation, he gained the street door and flung it open. Hathall and the woman were on the pavement edge, surrounded by their cases, waiting to hail a taxi.

Wexford flashed a glance at the car, caught Hutton's eye and raised his hand sharply, beckoning. Three of the car's doors opened simultaneously and the three policemen it had contained were on their feet, bounced on to the wet stone as if on springs. And then Hathall understood. He swung round to face them, his arm enclosing the woman in a protective but useless hold. The colour went out of his face, and in the light of the misted yellow lamps the jutting jaw, the sharp nose and the high forehead were greenish with terror and the final failure of his hopes. Wexford went up to him.

The woman said, 'We should have left last night, Bob,' and when he heard her accent, made strong by fear, he knew. He knew for sure. But he couldn't find his voice and, standing silent, he left it to Lovat to approach her and begin the words of the caution and the charge.

'Morag Grey ...'

She brought her knuckles to her trembling lips, and Wexford saw the small L-shaped scar on her forefinger as he had seen it in his dreams.

23

Christmas Eve.

They had all arrived and Wexford's house was full.
Upstairs, the two little grandsons were in bed. In
the kitchen Dora was again examining that turkey,
consulting Denise this time as to the all-important
question of whether to hang it up or lay it on the
oven shelf. In the living room Sheila and her sister
were dressing the tree while Burden's teenage
children subjected the record player, which had to
be in good order for the following day, to a rather
inexpert servicing. Burden had taken Wexford's
son-in-law down to the Dragon for a drink.

'The dining room for us then,' said Wexford
to his nephew. The table was already laid for
Christmas dinner, already decorated with a handsome

centerpiece. And the fire was laid too, as sacrosanct as the table, but Wexford put a match to the sticks. 'I shall get into trouble about that,' he said, 'but I don't care. I don't care about anything now I've found her, now *you*,' he added generously, 'and I have found her.'

'It was little or nothing I did,' said Howard. 'I never even found where she was living. Presumably, you know now?'

'In Pembridge Road itself,' said Wexford. 'He only had that miserable room but he paid the rent of a whole flat for her. No doubt, he loves her, though the last thing I want is to be sentimental about him.' He took a new bottle of whisky from the sideboard, poured a glass for Howard and then, recklessly, one for himself. 'Shall I tell you about it?'

'Is there much left to tell? Mike Burden's already filled me in on the identity of the woman, this Morag Grey. I tried to stop him. I knew you'd want to tell me yourself.'

'Mike Burden,' said his uncle as the fire began to crackle and blaze, 'had today off. I haven't seen him since I left him at London Airport yesterday afternoon. He hasn't filled you in, he doesn't know, unless – is it in the evening papers? The special court, I mean?'

'It wasn't in the early editions.'

'Then there is much left to tell.' Wexford drew the curtains against the fog which had returned in the afternoon. 'What did Mike say?'

'That it happened more or less the way you

guessed, the three of them in the pay-roll fraud. Wasn't it that way?'

'My theory,' Wexford said, 'left far too many loopholes.' He pulled his armchair closer to the fire. 'Good to relax, isn't it? Aren't you glad you haven't got to get your tailing gear on and go off up to West End Green?'

'I'll say it again, I did very little. But at least I don't deserve to be kept in suspense.'

'True, and I won't keep you in it. There was a pay-roll fraud all right. Hathall set up at least two fictitious accounts, and maybe more, soon after he joined Kidd's. He was pulling in a minimum of an extra thirty pounds a week for two years. But Morag Grey wasn't in on it. She wouldn't have helped anyone swindle a company. She was an honest woman. She was so honest she didn't even keep a pound note she found on an office floor, and so upright she wouldn't stay married to a man who'd stolen two pounds fifty. She couldn't have been in on it, still less have planned and collected from the Mary Lewis account because Hathall didn't meet her till the March. She was only at Kidd's for a couple of weeks and that was three months before Hathall left.'

'But Hathall was in love with her, surely? You said so yourself. And what other motive ...?'

'Hathall was in love with his wife. Oh, I know we decided he'd acquired amorous tastes, but what real evidence did we have of that?' With a slight self-consciousness too well covered for Howard to detect, Wexford said, 'If he was so susceptible, why did he reject the advances of a certain very attractive neighbour of his? Why did he give everyone who knew him the impression of being an obsessively devoted husband?'

'You tell me,' Howard grinned. 'You'll be saying in a minute that Morag Grey didn't kill Angela Hathall.'

'That's right. She didn't. Angela Hathall killed Morag Grey.'

A wail rose from the record player in the next room. Small feet scuttled across the floor above and there was a violent crash from the kitchen. The noise drowned Howard's low exclamation.

'I was pretty surprised myself,' Wexford went on casually. 'I suppose I guessed when I found out yesterday about Morag Grey being so honest and only being at Kidd's for such a short while. Then when we arrested them and I heard her Australian accent I knew.'

Howard shook his head slowly in astonishment and wonder rather than disbelief. 'But the identification, Reg? How could he hope to get away with it?'

'He did get away with it for fifteen months. You see, the secretive isolated life they led in order to make the pay-roll scheme work was in their favour when they planned this murder. It wouldn't have done for Angela to get well known in case she was recognized as not being Mrs Lewis or Mrs Carter when she went to make withdrawals from those accounts. Hardly a soul knew her even by sight. Mrs Lake did, of course, and so did her cousin, Mark

Somerset, but who on earth would have called on them to identify the body? The natural person was Angela's husband. And just in case there was any doubt, he took his mother with him, taking care she should see the body first. Angela had dressed Morag in her own clothes, those very clothes she was wearing on the only previous occasion her mother-in-law had seen her. That was a fine piece of psychology, Howard, thought up, I'm sure, by Angela who planned all the intricacies of this business. It was old Mrs Hathall who phoned us, old Mrs Hathall who put doubt out of court by telling us her daughter-in-law had been found dead in Bury Cottage.

'Angela started cleaning the place weeks ahead to clean off *her own fingerprints*. No wonder she had rubber gloves and dusting gloves. It wouldn't have been too difficult a task, seeing she was alone all week without Hathall there to leave his own prints about. And if we queried such extreme cleanliness, what better reason for it than that she was getting the cottage perfect for old Mrs Hathall's visit?'

'Then the handprint and the L-shaped scar were hers?'

'Of course.' Wexford drank his whisky slowly, making it last. 'The prints we thought were hers were Morag's. The hair in the brush we thought was hers was Morag's. She must have brushed the dead girl's hair – nasty, that. The coarser dark hairs were Angela's. She didn't have to clean the car in the garage or at Wood Green. She could have cleaned it at any time she chose in the previous week.'

'But why did she leave that one print?'

'I think I can guess at that. On the morning of the day Morag died, Angela was up early getting on with her cleaning. She was cleaning the bathroom, had perhaps taken off her rubber gloves and was about to put on the others to polish the floor, when the phone rang. Mrs Lake rang to ask if she could come over and pick the miracle plums. And Angela, naturally nervous, steadied herself with her bare hand on the side of the bath when she got up to answer the phone.

'Morag Grey spoke, and doubtless read, Gaelic. Hathall must have known that. So Angela found out her address – they would have been keeping a close eye on her – and wrote to her, or more probably called on her, to ask if she would give her some assistance into the research she was doing into Celtic languages. Morag, a domestic servant, can only have been flattered. And she was poor too, she needed money. This, I think, was the good job she spoke of to her neighbour, and she gave up her cleaning work at this time, going on to the Social Security until Angela was ready for her to start.'

'But didn't she know Angela?'

'Why should she? Angela would have given her a false name, and I see no reason why she should have known Hathall's address. On the nineteenth of September Angela drove over to Myringham Old Town, collected her and drove her to Bury Cottage for a discussion on their future work. She took Morag upstairs to wash or go to the loo or comb her hair.

258

And there she strangled her, Howard, with her own gilt snake necklace.

'After that it was simple. Dress Morag in the red shirt and the jeans, imprint a few mobile objects with her fingerprints, brush her hair. Gloves on, take the car down that tunnel of a lane, away to London. Stay a night or two in an hotel till she could find a room, wait for time to go by till Hathall could join her.'

'But why, Reg? Why kill her?'

'She was an honest woman and she found out what Hathall was up to. She was no fool, Howard, but rather one of those people who have potential but lack drive. Both her former employer and her mother said she was a cut above the kind of work she was doing. Her feckless husband dragged her down. Who knows? Maybe she would have had the ability to advise a *genuine* etymologist on demotic Gaelic, and maybe she thought this was her chance, now she was rid of Grey, to better herself. Angela Hathall, when you come to think of it, is a very good psychologist.'

'I see all that,' said Howard, 'but how did Morag find out about the pay-roll fraud?'

'That,' Wexford said frankly, 'I don't know – yet. I'd guess Hathall stayed late one evening while she was working there, and I'd guess she overheard a phone conversation he had with Angela on that occasion. Perhaps Angela had suggested a false address to him and he called her to check up he'd got it right before he fed it into the computer. Don't forget Angela was the mainspring behind all this.

You couldn't have been more right when you said she'd influenced and corrupted him. Hathall is just the sort of man to think of a cleaner as no more than a piece of furniture. But even if he'd spoken guardedly, that name, Mrs Mary Lewis, and that address, 19 Maynnot Way, would have alerted Morag. It was just down the road from where she and her husband lived and she knew no Mary Lewis lived there. And if, after that call, Hathall immediately began to feed the computer ...'

'She blackmailed him?'

'I doubt it. She was an honest woman. But she'd have queried it, on the spot perhaps. Maybe she merely told him she'd overheard what he'd said and there was no Mary Lewis there, and if he'd seemed flustered – my God, you should see him when he's flustered! – she could have asked more and more questions until she had some hazy idea of what was actually going on.'

'They killed her for *that*?'

Wexford nodded. 'To you and me it seems a wretched motive. But to them? They would ever after have been in a panic of fear, for if Hathall's swindle were uncovered he'd lose his job, lose his new job at Marcus Flower, never get another job in the one field he was trained for. You have to remember what a paranoid pair they were. They expected to be persecuted and hounded, they suspected even the innocent and harmless of having a down on them.'

'You weren't innocent and harmless, Reg,' said Howard quietly.

'No, and perhaps I'm the only person who has ever truly persecuted Robert Hathall.' Wexford raised his almost empty glass. 'Happy Christmas,' he said. 'I shan't let Hathall's loss of liberty cloud the season for me. If anyone deserves to lose it, he does. Shall we join the others? I think I heard Mike come in with my son-in-law.'

The tree had been dressed. Sheila was jiving with John Burden to the thumping cacophony that issued from the record player. Having restored a sleepy little boy to his bed for the third time, Sylvia was wrapping the last of the presents, one of Kidd's Kits for Kids, a paint-box, a geographical globe, a picture book, a toy car. Wexford put an arm round his wife and an arm round Pat Burden and kissed them under the mistletoe. Laughing, he put his hand out to the globe and spun it. Three times it circled on its axis before Burden saw the point, and then he said:

'It does move. You were right. He did do it.'

'Well, you were right too,' said Wexford. 'He didn't murder his wife.' Seeing Burden's look of incredulity, he added, 'And now I suppose I shall have to tell the story all over again.'

Read on for the first chapter of the next
Wexford Case novel

ruth
rendell

A SLEEPING LIFE

1

Home early for once. Maybe he'd start getting home early regularly now August had begun, the silly season. Criminals as well as the law-abiding take their holidays in August. As he turned the car into his own road, Wexford remembered his grandsons would be there. Good. It would be light for another three hours, and he'd take Robin and Ben down to the river. Robin was always on about the river because his mother had read *The Wind in the Willows* to him, and his great desire was to see a water rat swimming.

Sylvia's car was parked outside the house. Odd, thought Wexford. He'd understood Dora was having the boys for the afternoon as well as the evening and that they'd be staying the night. As he edged his own car past his daughter's into the drive, she came running out of the house with a screaming Ben in her arms and six-year-old Robin looking truculent at her heels. Robin rushed up to his grandfather.

'You promised we could see the water rat!'

'So you can as far as I'm concerned and if there's one about. I thought you were staying the night.'

Sylvia's face was crimson, with rage or perhaps just from haste. It was very hot.

'Well, they're not. Thanks to my dear husband, nobody's going anywhere even though it does happen to be our wedding anniversary. Will you shut up, Ben! He's bringing a client home for dinner instead, if you please, and I of course as usual have to be the one to do the cooking and fetch the kids.'

'Leave them here,' said Wexford. 'Why not?'

'Yes, leave us here,' Robin shouted. '*Go on.*'

'Oh, no, that's out of the question. Why do you have to encourage them, Dad? I'm taking them home and Neil can have the pleasure of putting them to bed for once.'

She thrust both children into the car and drove off. The windows of the car were all open, and the yells of the two little boys, for Robin had begun to back his brother up, vied with the roar of the ill-treated engine. Wexford shrugged and went indoors. Some sort of scene had evidently been taking place, but he knew his wife better than to suppose she would be much disturbed by it. True to his expectations, she was sitting placidly in the living room watching the tail end of a children's programme on television. A great many books had been pulled out of the shelves, and on a tower block of them sat a teddy bear.

'What's got into Sylvia?'

'Women's Lib,' said Dora Wexford. 'If Neil wants to bring a client home he ought to cook the meal. He ought to come home in the afternoon and clean the house and lay the table. She's taken the children home for the sole purpose of getting him to put them to bed. And she's taking care to stir them up on the way to make sure he has a hard time of it.'

'God. I always thought she was quite a sensible girl.'

'She's got a bee in her bonnet about it. It's been going on for months. You are the people, we are the others. You are the masters, we are the chattels.'

'Why haven't you told me about any of this?'

Dora switched off the television. 'You've been busy. You wouldn't have wanted to listen to all this nonsense when you got home. I've been getting it every day.'

Wexford raised his eyebrows. 'It's nonsense?'

'Well, not entirely, of course. Men still do have a better time of it in this world than women, it's still a man's world. I can understand she doesn't like being stuck at home with the boys, wasting her life, as she puts it, while Neil gets more and more successful in his career.' Dora smiled. 'And she says she got more A Levels than he did. I can understand she gets bored when people come and the men talk to Neil about architecture and the women talk to her about polishing the bedroom furniture. Oh, I can *understand* it.'

Her husband looked hard at her. 'You feel that way too?'

'Never you mind,' said Dora, laughing now. 'Let's forget our rather tiresome child. You're so early we might go out somewhere after we've eaten. Would you like to?'

'Love to.' He hesitated, said quickly, 'It's not threatening their marriage, is it? I've always thought of them as being so happy together.'

'We have to hope it'll pass. Anything we do or say would only make things worse, wouldn't it?'

'Of course. Now where shall we go? Cinema? Or how about the open-air theatre at Sewingbury?'

Before she could give him an answer, the phone rang.

'Sylvia,' she said. 'She's realized Ben left his teddy. You get it, darling. Oh, and Reg . . .? Would you say we'll drop it in on our way? I can't stand another session of the wounded wives tonight.'

Wexford lifted the receiver. It wasn't his daughter. Dora knew it wasn't even before he spoke. She knew that look. All he said was 'Yes' and 'Sure, I will', but she knew. He hung up and said. 'They don't all go on holiday in August. A body in a field not half a mile from here.'

'It is . . .?'

'Not one of the people,' said her husband dryly. 'One of the others.' He tightened the tie he had loosened, rolled down his shirtsleeves. 'I'll have to go straightaway. What'll you do? Stir up the telly so I have a hard time of it putting it to rights? You must regret marrying me.'

'No, but I'm working on it.'

Wexford laughed, kissed her and drove back the way he had come.

Kingsmarkham is a sizeable town somewhere in the middle of Sussex, much built-up now on the Stowerton and Sewingbury sides, though open unspoilt country still remains at its northern end. There the High Street becomes the Pomfret Road, and there the pinewoods of Cheriton Forest clothe the hills.

Forest Road is the last street in the area to bear the postal address Kingsmarkham. It debouches directly from the Pomfret Road, but to reach it most of its few residents take the short cut from the end of the High Street by footpath across a field. Wexford parked his car at the point in Forest Road where this footpath entered it as an alley near the boundary fence of a pair of houses called Carlyle Villas. He swung into the alley and followed the footpath along a high privet hedge that bounded allotments. About a hundred yards ahead of him he could see a group of men gathered at the edge of a little copse.

Inspector Michael Burden was among them and so was Dr Crocker, the police doctor, and a couple of photographers. As Wexford approached, Burden came up to him and said something in a low voice. Wexford nodded. Without looking at the body, he went up to Detective Loring who stood a little apart with a young man who looked pale and shaken.

'Mr Parker?'

'That's right.'

'I understand you found the body?'

Parker nodded. 'Well, my son did.'

He couldn't have been more than twenty-five himself.

'A *child*?' said Wexford.

'He doesn't realize. I hope not. He's only six.'

They sat down on a wooden seat the council had put there for pensioners to rest on. 'Tell me what happened.'

'I'd taken him round to my sister's, give the wife a bit of a break while she was putting the other two to bed. I live in one of the bungalows in Forest Road, Bella Vista, the one with the green roof. We were coming back, along the path here, and Nicky was playing with a ball. It went in the long grass under the hedge and he went to look for it. He said, "Dad, there's a lady down there." I sort of knew, I don't know how. I went and looked and I – well, I know I shouldn't have, but I sort of pulled her coat over her chest. Nicky, you see, he's only six, there was – well, blood, a mess.'

'I do see,' said Wexford. 'You didn't move anything else?'

Parker shook his head. 'I told Nicky the lady was ill and we'd go home and phone the doctor. I said she'd be all right. I don't think he realized. I hope not. I got him home and phoned your people. Honestly, I wouldn't have touched her if I'd been on my own.'

'This was an exception, Mr Parker.' Wexford smiled at him. 'I'd have done the same in your place.'

'He won't have to . . .? I mean, there'll be an inquest, won't there? I mean, I'll have to go, I know that, but . . .'

'No, no. Good God, no. Get off home now and we'll see you again later. Thanks for your help.'

Parker got up off the seat, glanced at the photographers, the huddle round the body, then turned round. 'It's not for me to . . . Well, I mean, I do know who she is. Perhaps you don't . . .'

'No, we don't yet. Who is she?'

'Well, a Miss Comfrey. She didn't actually live here, her dad lives here.' Parker pointed back down the path. 'Carlyle Villas, the one with the blue paint. She must have been stopping there. Her dad's in hospital. He's an old man, he broke his hip, and she must have come down to see him.'

'Thanks Mr Parker.'

Wexford crossed the sandy path, and Burden stepped aside for him to look down at the body. It was that of a middle-aged woman, biggish and gaunt. The face was coated with heavy make-up, clotted scarlet on the mouth, streaky blue on the crêpe eyelids, a ghastly ochreish layer on the planes of cheek and forehead. The grey eyes were wide and staring, and in them Wexford thought he saw – it must be his imagination – a sardonic gleam, a glare, even in death, of scorn.

A fringe of dark hair just showed under a tightly tied blue headscarf. The body was clothed in a blue and pink printed dress of some synthetic material, and the matching jacket had been drawn across the bodice. One of the high-heeled shoes had come off and hung suspended on a tangle of brambles. Across the hips lay a large scarlet handbag. There were no rings on the hands, no watch on either wrist, but a heavy necklace of red glass beads round the neck, and the nails, though short, were painted the same scarlet.

He knelt down and opened the handbag, covering his fingers with his handkerchief. Inside was a key ring with three keys on it, a box of matches, a packet of king-size cigarettes from which four had been smoked, a lipstick, an old-fashioned powder compact, a wallet, in the bottom of the bag some loose change. No purse. No letters or documents. The wallet, which was an expensive new one of black leather, contained forty-two pounds. She hadn't been killed for the money she had on her.

There was nothing to give him a clue to her address, her occupation or even her identity. No credit card, no bank card, no cheque book.

He closed the bag and parted her jacket. The bodice of the dress was black with clotted blood, but plainly discernible in the dark matted mass were two cuts, the outward evidence of stab wounds.

The Monster in the Box

Ruth Rendell

Wexford had almost made up his mind that he would never again set eyes on Eric Targo's short, muscular figure. And yet there he was, back in Kingsmarkham, still with that cocky, strutting walk. Years earlier, when Wexford was a young police officer, a woman called Elsie Carroll had been found strangled in her bedroom. Although many still had their suspicions that her husband was guilty, no one was convicted.

Another woman was strangled shortly afterwards, and every personal and professional instinct told Wexford that the killer was still at large. And it was Eric Targo. A psychopath who would kill again . . .

As the Chief Inspector investigates a new case, Ruth Rendell looks back to the beginning of Wexford's career, even to his courtship of the woman who would later become his wife. The past is a haunted place, with clues and passions that leave an indelible imprint on the here and now.

A WEXFORD CASE NOVEL

Some Lie and Some Die

Ruth Rendell

Fame comes at a price

When the body of a brutally beaten girl is found in a quarry during a hedonistic hippy festival at Sundays near Kingsmarkham, Wexford is first on the scene. The victim's face has been pulped by the back-end of a bottle, but who, in this atmosphere of peace and love, could be capable of such violence?

The body is that of local girl turned stripper Dawn Stonor, but it is the unlikely link between this ill-fated woman and the mysterious folk-singer Zeno Vedast that pique Wexford's interest.

Through a web of lies and deceit Wexford uncovers a history of love and hate that began years earlier, and he realises that never has he witnessed a murder of such desperate passion . . .

'Ruth Rendell is streets ahead'
Sunday Telegraph

arrow books

A WEXFORD CASE NOVEL

A Sleeping Life

Ruth Rendell

Death is always solitary. For some, so is life . . .

On a sultry August evening, the bloody body of a middle-aged
woman is discovered beneath a hedge by a small boy.

There are two things that surprise Wexford about the murder scene.
One, that the only contents of the woman's handbag are some keys
and a wallet containing nothing but some money. And two, how
even in death, her deathly grey eyes possess a scornful glare.

The woman turns out to be Rhoda Comfrey, but there's no murder
weapon, no apparent motive, and no one who actually cares she's
died. Wexford's only hunch is that the clues to her murder must lie
in her solitary London life. But her existence there becomes
frustratingly impossible to trace.

'Intelligent, well-written, and with a surprising twist at the end'
Times Literary Supplement

arrow books

A WEXFORD CASE NOVEL

Means of Evil and Other Stories

Ruth Rendell

Innocence is in the eye of the beholder

What connects a kidnapped baby, a woman's body left to rot in a cove in Yugoslavia, a suspicious suicide and the century-old case of a wife who poisons her husband? The answer: Wexford.

In the first of five cases, Wexford is brought in to deal with a distraught mother whose baby girl has been swapped with an unknown baby boy. When a local priest discovers the missing baby, safe and sound, on the church steps, the hunt for the missing girl is quickly over.

Mother and daughter are happily reunited, but the mystery of the baby boy remains unsolved. Then Wexford discovers Paddy Jasper has returned to Kingsmarkham, a man previously investigated by Wexford for violently abusing a child. Now Wexford fears this reunion may not be as happy as the last . . .

'Full of ideas . . . as a page-turner there are few who can match Ruth'
Colin Dexter

arrow books

A WEXFORD CASE NOVEL

Put On By Cunning

Ruth Rendell

A legacy to die for

The tragic death of Manuel Camargue, Kingsmarkham's very own celebrity flautist, is met with a ruling of misadventure. But when, after an absence of nineteen years, Camargue's entrancing daughter Natalie reappears, Dinah, his fiancée, goes to Wexford for help.

Dinah believes Natalie is not who she claims to be. Knowing there is a large inheritance at stake, Wexford begins to investigate.

But then events take a gruesome twist and now, more than ever, Wexford must establish Natalie's true identity.

'Ruth Rendell exercises a grip as relentless as an anaconda's'
Guardian

arrow books

ALSO AVAILABLE IN ARROW

Portobello

Ruth Rendell

'Found in Chepstow Villas, a sum of money between eighty and a hundred and sixty pounds. Anyone who has lost such a sum of money should apply to the phone number below.'

The chance discovery by Eugene Wren of an envelope filled with banknotes would link the lives of a number of very different people – each with their own obsessions, problems, dreams and despairs. It would also set in motion a chain of events that lead to arson and murder.

'It is Rendell's superb sense of place that counts. She makes you smell the excitement and the desperation. *Portobello* is as brilliant as anything she has ever written' *Evening Standard*

'Rendell has a Dickensian empathy, informed by a prodigious love of London life. Her account, bursting with colour and vitality, is a treat to read'
Independent

arrow books